TO BE TAKEN AT NIGHT

NOT TO BE TAKEN AT NIGHT

Thirteen Classic Tales of Mystery and the Supernatural

Selected by

John Robert Colombo & Michael Richardson

RR
RAVETTE BOOKS

First published by Ravette Books Limited, 1988

Printed and bound in Great Britain
for Ravette Books Limited,
3 Glenside Estate, Star Road, Patridge Green
Horsham, West Sussex RH18 8RA
by Cox & Wyman Ltd, Reading

ISBN 0 948456 77 9

Dedicated to Ruth and Jeannie,
companions in terror

CONTENTS

PREFACE

"The oldest and strongest emotion of mankind is fear, and the oldest and strongest kind of fear is fear of the unknown." So wrote H. P. Lovecraft about fear and its presentation in fiction. Yet frightening tales of the unknown are irresistible – people of all cultures and all ages are enticed and enthralled by the inexplicable, the eerie, and the horrific.

In the past, most horror stories were set in certain traditional locales: the crumbling castle, complete with moonlit battlements and dank oubliettes; the isolated manse, abandoned and boarded up since "the accident"; the bleak moor with its wailing winds and rotting gibbet. . . But these scenes are alien to our way of life and so – paradoxically – they are not so much alarming as comforting.

What of the people of today. . . in modern houses and office buildings, split-levels and shopping precincts, rural towns and fishing villages? Have we succeeded in exiling the bizarre and the baffling from our lives? Have we grown too staid and unimaginative to invent harrowing tales of the dark powers? Are we too prosperous and complacement to derive the slightest *frisson* from the unknown?

Not at all. The unknown has not vanished; it has merely shed its reassuring old accoutrements and moved onto the modern scene. It prowls the familar streets where we argue over football teams and local politics, skulks in the parks, stalks the busy junctions of our cities and waving fields. It has taken a different and more psychological form, but that is only right; after all, it is not places that are haunted, but people. And perhaps we are more haunted now than ever before, for we are losing our childish confidence, our trust in unending technology; we are becoming somewhat wary, if also curious, about the mysterious forces both around us and within us. We are also beginning to realize that we are not, and never will be, masters of the twentieth century; that our urbanized life-styles are not entirely satisfying; that all our inventions will never lay to rest the disturbed spirits that haunt our psyches.

We have turned to the best contemporary writers – some known for their short stories, others better known for their novels, plays, or poetry – to see what excursions they have made into the unknown. Some of them have written of the supernatural; some have delved into the darker side of our own psychology; some have explored those strange boundaries of normal and paranormal, real and surreal. But all these writers have succeeded in cutting out from under our feet the *terra firma* of "what is", and have left us suspended in the frightful void of "what ought not to be".

Place yourself, then, in the hands of these thirteen masters of fear; let them carry you off to their weird and fascinating worlds. And if you are tempted to comfort yourself with the thought that this is, after all, only fiction, you may with profit ponder the question posed by Sir Devendra P. Varma, "Modern civilization consists of the living dead. Why then should we object to the dead living?"

The editors are pleased to acknowledge the advice and assistance so freely granted them by friends and colleagues. David Kotin and Philip Singer of the North York Public Library System rendered signal service, as did Doris Mehegan and David Aylward of the Spaced Out Library in the Toronto Public Library System. Michael Richardson feels especially indebted to David Cronenberg, Jeff Plewman, Gary Topp, and Elwy Yost for feeding his sense of horror. John Robert Colombo gratefully acknowledges the help of Sharon Anderson, Chester D. Cuthbert, Doug Fetherling, Bob Hadji, Geoff Hancock, Bill Howell, Anna Porter, Bruce Robbins, and Stephen Scobie, as well as the assistance of the Explorations Programme of the Canada Council. Both editors are indebted to the Ontario Arts Council.

NOT TO BE TAKEN AT NIGHT

ROBERTSON DAVIES

THE CAT THAT WENT TO TRINITY

Robertson Davies—novelist, playwright, essayist, editor, and all-round man of letters—is acclaimed for his social comedies and the imaginative novels of the Deptford trilogy: Fifth Business, The Manticore, *and* World of Wonders. *He has a great interest in tales of the supernatural; as he once wrote, "There must be something about the spirit of our age which is uncongenial to belief in ghosts. Surely it is a little conceited of us to suppose that we are the only spiritual inhabitants of this world? But that appears to be the common belief, and one of its lesser evils is that it robs us of a good supply of ghost stories."*

As Master of Massey College, University of Toronto, he treated the College to a series of uncanny tales at the annual Gaudy nights; the following story, which comes from that series, is a wonderful mixture of fantasy, satire, and good old-fashioned Gothic horror.

EVERY Autumn when I meet my new classes, I look them over to see if there are any pretty girls in them. This is not a custom peculiar to me: all professors do it. A pretty girl is something on which I can rest my eyes with pleasure while another student is reading a carefully researched but uninspiring paper.

This year, in my seminar on the Gothic Novel, there was an exceptionally pretty girl, whose name was Elizabeth Lavenza. I thought it a coincidence that this should also be the name of the heroine of one of the novels we were about to study —no less a work than Mary Shelley's celebrated romance *Frankenstein*. When I mentioned it to her she brushed it aside as of no significance.

"I was born in Geneva," said she, "where lots of people are called Lavenza."

Nevertheless, it lingered in my mind, and I mentioned it to one of my colleagues, who is a celebrated literary critic.

"You have coincidence on the brain," he said. "Ever since you wrote that book—*Fourth Dimension* or whatever it was called—you've talked about nothing else. Forget it."

I tried, but I couldn't forget it. It troubled me even more after I had met the new group of Junior Fellows in this College, for one of them was young Einstein, who was studying Medical Biophysics. He was a brilliant young man, who came to us with glowing recommendations; some mention was made of a great-uncle of his, an Albert Einstein, whose name meant nothing to me, though it appeared to have special significance in the scientific world. It was young Mr. Einstein's given names that roused an echo in my consciousness, for he was called Victor Frank.

For those among you who have not been reading Gothic

Novels lately, I may explain that in Mrs. Shelley's book *Frankenstein, or The Modern Prometheus*, the hero's name is also Victor, and the girl he loved was Elizabeth Lavenza. This richness of coincidence might trouble a mind less disposed to such reflection than mine. I held my peace, for I had been cowed by what my friend the literary critic had said. But I was dogged by apprehension, for I know the disposition of the atmosphere of Massey College to constellate extraordinary elements. Thus, cowed and dogged, I kept my eyes open for what might happen.

It was no more than a matter of days when Fate added another figure to this coincidental pattern, and Fate's instrument was none other than my wife. It is our custom to entertain the men of the College to dinner, in small groups, and my wife invites a few girls to each of these occasions to lighten what might otherwise be a too exclusively academic atmosphere. The night that Frank Einstein appeared in our drawing-room he maintained his usual reserved—not to say morose—demeanour until Elizabeth Lavenza entered the room. Their meeting was, in one sense, a melodramatic cliché. But we must remember that things become clichés because they are of frequent occurrence, and powerful impact. Their eyes met across the room. His glance was electric; hers ecstatic. The rest of the company seemed to part before them as he moved to her side. He never left it all evening. She had eyes for no other. From time to time his eyes rose in ardour, while hers fell in modest transport. This rising and falling of eyes was so portentously and swooningly apparent that one or two of our senior guests felt positively unwell, as though aboard ship. My heart sank. My wife's, on the contrary, was uplifted. As I passed her during the serving of the meal I hissed, "This is Fate." "There is no armour against Fate," she hissed in return. It is a combination of words not easily hissed, but she hissed it.

We had an unusually fine Autumn, as you will recall, and there was hardly a day that I did not see Frank and Elizabeth sitting on one of the benches in the quad, sometimes talking, but usually looking deep into each other's eyes, their foreheads touching. They did it so much that they both became slightly cross-eyed, and my dismay mounted. I determined if humanly possible to avert some disastrous outcome (for I assure you that my intuition and my knowledge of the curious atmosphere of this College both oppressed me with boding) and I did all that lay in my power. I heaped work on Elizabeth Lavenza; I demanded the ultimate from her in reading of the Gothic Novel, as a means both of keeping her from Frank, and of straightening her vision.

Alas, how puny are our best efforts to avert a foreordained event! One day I saw Frank in the quad, sitting on the bench alone, reading a book. Pretending nonchalance, I sat beside him. "And what are you reading, Mr. Einstein?" I said in honeyed tones.

Taciturn as always, he held out the book for me to see. It was *Frankenstein*. "Liz said I ought to read it," he said.

"And what do you make of it?" said I, for I am always interested in the puny efforts of art to penetrate the thoroughly scientific mind. His answer astonished me.

"Not bad at all," said he. "The Medical Biophysics aspect of the plot is very old-fashioned, of course. I mean when the hero makes that synthetic human being out of scraps from slaughter-houses. We could do better than that now. A lot better," he added, and I thought he seemed to be brooding on nameless possibilities. I decided to change the line of our conversation. I began to talk about the College, and some of the successes and failures we had met with in the past.

Among the failures I mentioned our inability to keep a College Cat. In the ten years of our existence we have had several cats here, but not one of them has remained with us. They all run away, and there is strong evidence that they all go to Trinity. I thought at one time that they must be Anglican cats, and they objected to our ecumenical chapel. I went to the length of getting a Persian cat, raised in the Zoroastrian faith, but it only lasted two days. There is a fine Persian rug in Trinity Chapel. Our most recent cat had been christened Episcopuss, in the hope that this thoroughly Anglican title would content it;

furthermore, the Lionel Massey fund provided money to treat the cat to a surgical operation which is generally thought to lift a cat's mind above purely sectarian considerations. But it, too, left us for Trinity. Rationalists in the College suggested that Trinity has more, and richer, refuse than we have, but I still believe our cats acted on religious impulse.

As I spoke of these things Frank Einstein became more animated than I had ever known him. "I get it," he said; "you want a cat that has been specifically programmed for Massey. An ecumenical cat, highly intelligent so that it prefers graduates to undergraduates, and incapable of making messes in the Round Room. With a few hours of computer time it oughtn't to be too difficult."

I looked into his eyes—though from a greater distance than was usual to Elizabeth Lavenza—and what I saw there caused a familiar shudder to convulse my entire being. It is the shudder I feel when I know, for a certainty, that Massey College is about to be the scene of yet another macabre event.

Nevertheless, in the pressure of examinations and lectures, I forgot my uneasiness, and might perhaps have dismissed the matter from my mind if two further interrelated circumstances—I dare not use the word coincidence in this case—had not aroused my fears again. One autumn morning, reading *The Globe and Mail*, my eye was caught by an item, almost lost at the bottom of a column, which bore the heading "Outrage at Pound"; it appeared that two masked bandits, a man and a woman, had held up the keeper of the pound at gun-point, while seizing no less than twelve stray cats. Later that same day I saw Frank and Elizabeth coming through the College gate, carrying a large and heavy sack. From the sack dripped a substance which I recognized, with horror, as blood. I picked up a little of it on the tip of my finger; a hasty corpuscle count confirmed my suspicion that the blood was not human.

Night after night in the weeks that followed, I crept down to my study to look across the quad and see if a light was burning in Frank Einstein's room. Invariably it was so. And one morning, when I had wakened early and was standing on my balcony, apostrophizing the dawn, Elizabeth Lavenza stole past me from the College's main gate, her face marked, not by those lineaments of slaked desire so common among our visitors at such an hour, but by the pallor and fatigue of one well-nigh exhausted by intellectual work of the most demanding sort.

The following night I awoke from sleep at around two o'clock with a terrifying apprehension that something was happening in the College which I should investigate. Shouts, the sound of loud music, the riot of late revellers—these things do not particularly disturb me, but there is a quality of deep silence which I know to be the accompaniment of evil. Wearily and reluctantly I rose, wrapped myself in a heavy dressing-gown, and made my way into the quadrangle and there—yes, it was as I had feared—the eerie gleam from Frank Einstein's room was the only light to guide me. For there was a thick fog hanging over the University, and even the cruel light through the arrow-slits of the Robarts Library and the faery radiance from OISE were hidden.

Up to his room I climbed, and tapped on the door. It had not been locked, and my light knock caused it to swing open and there—never can I forget my shock and revulsion at what I saw!—there were Frank and Elizabeth crouched over a table upon which lay an ensanguined form. I burst upon them.

"What bloody feast is this?" I shouted. "Monsters, fiends, cannibals, what do I behold?"

"Shhh," said Elizabeth; "Frank's busy."

"I'm making your cat," said Frank.

"Cat," I shrieked, almost beside myself; "that is no cat. It's as big as a donkey. What cat are you talking about?"

"The Massey College cat," said Frank. "And it is going to be the greatest cat you have ever seen."

I shall not trouble you with a detailed report of the conversation that followed. What emerged was this: Frank, beneath the uncommunicative exterior of a scientist, had a kindly heart, and he had been touched by the unlucky history of Massey College and its cats. "What you said was," said he to me, "that the College never seemed to get the right cat. To you, with your simple, emotional, literary approach to the problem, this was an insuperable difficulty: to my finely organized biophysical sensibility, it was simply a matter of discovering what kind of cat was wanted, and producing it. Not by the outmoded method of selective breeding, but by the direct creation of the Ideal College Cat, or ICC as I came to think of it. Do you remember that when you talked to me about it I was reading the crazy book Liz was studying with you, about the fellow who made a man? Do you remember what he said? 'Whence did the principle of life proceed? It was a bold question, and one which has ever been considered as a mystery; yet with how many things are we upon the brink of becoming acquainted, if cowardice or carelessness did not restrain our enquiries.' That was written in 1818. Since then the principle of life has become quite well known, but most scientists are afraid to work on the knowledge they have. You remember that the fellow in the book decided to make a man, but he found the work too fiddly if he made a man of ordinary size, so he decided to make a giant. Me too. A cat of ordinary size is a nuisance, so I decided to multiply the dimensions by twelve. And like the fellow in the book I got my materials and went to work. Here is your cat, about three-quarters finished."

The fatal weakness, the tragic flaw, in my character is foolish good-nature, and that, combined with an uninformed but lively scientific curiosity, led me into what was, I now perceive, a terrible mistake. I was so interested in what Frank was doing that I allowed him to go ahead, and instead of sleeping at nights I crept up to his room, where Frank and Elizabeth allowed me, after I had given my promise not to interfere or touch anything, to sit in a corner and watch them. Those weeks were perhaps the most intensely lived that I have ever known. Beneath my eyes the ICC grew and took form. By day the carcass was kept in the freezer at Rochdale, where Elizabeth had a room; each night Frank warmed it up and set to work.

The ICC had many novel features which distinguished it from the ordinary domestic cat. Not only was it as big as twelve ordinary cats; it had twelve times the musculature. Frank said proudly than when it was finished it would be able to jump right over the College buildings. Another of its beauties was that it possessed a novel means of elimination. The trouble with all cats is that they seem to be housebroken, but in moments of stress or laziness they relapse into an intolerable bohemianism which creates problems for the cleaning staff. In a twelve-power cat this could be a serious defect. But Frank's cat was made with a small shovel on the end of its tail with which it could, once a week, remove its own ashes and deposit them behind the College in the parking-space occupied by *The Varsity*, where, it was assumed, they would never be noticed. I must hasten to add that the cat was made to sustain itself on a diet of waste-paper, of which we have plenty, and that what it produced in the manner I have described was not unlike confetti.

But the special beauty of the ICC was that it could talk. This, in the minds of Frank and Elizabeth, was its great feature as a College pet. Instead of mewing monotonously when stroked, it would be able to enter into conversation with the College men, and as we pride ourselves on being a community of scholars, it was to be provided with a class of conversation and a vocabulary, infinitely superior to that of, for instance, a parrot.

This was Elizabeth's special care, and because she was by this time deep in my course on the Gothic Novel she decided, as a compliment to me, to so program the cat that it would speak in the language appropriate to that *genre* of literature. I was not so confident about this refinement as were Frank and Elizabeth, for I knew more about Gothic Novels than they, and have sometimes admitted to myself that they can be wordy. But as I have told you, I was a party to this great adventure only in the character of a spectator, and I was not to interfere. So I held my peace, hoping that the cat would, in the fulness of time, do the same.

At last the great night came, when the cat was to be invested with life. I sat in my corner, my eyes fixed upon the form which Frank was gradually melting out with Elizabeth's electric hair-dryer. It was a sight to strike awe into the boldest heart.

I never dared to make my doubts about the great experiment known to Frank and Elizabeth, but I may tell you that my misgivings were many and acute. I am a creature of my time in that I fully understand that persons of merely aesthetic bias and training, like myself, should be silent in the presence of men of science, who know best about everything. But it was plain to me that the ICC was hideous. Not only was it the size of twelve cats, but the skins of twelve cats had been made to serve as its outer envelope. Four of these cats had been black, four were white, and four were of a marmalade colour. Frank, who liked things to be orderly, had arranged them so that the cat was piebald in mathematically exact squares. Because no ordinary cat's eyes would fit into the huge skull the eyes of a goat had been obtained—I dared not ask how—and as everyone knows, a goat's eyes are flat and have an uncanny oblong pupil. The teeth had been secured at a bargain rate from a denturist, and as I looked at them I knew why dentists say that these people must be kept in check. The tail, with the shovel at the end of it, was disagreeably naked. Its whiskers were like knitting needles. Indeed, the whole appearance of the cat was monstrous and diabolical. In the most exact sense of the words, it was the damnedest thing you ever saw. But Frank had a mind above appearances and to Elizabeth, so beautiful herself, whatever Frank did was right.

The moment had arrived when this marvel of science was to be set going. I know that Frank was entirely scientific, but to my old-fashioned eye he looked like an alchemist as, with his dressing-gown floating around him, he began to read formulae out of a notebook, and Elizabeth worked switches and levers at his command. Suddenly there was a flash, of lightning it seemed to me, and I knew that we had launched the ICC upon its great adventure.

"Come here and look," said Frank. I crept forward, half-afraid yet half-elated that I should be witness to such a triumph of medical biophysics. I leaned over the frightful creature, restraining my revulsion. Slowly, dreamily, the goat's eyes opened and focussed upon me.

"My Creator!" screamed the cat in a very loud voice, that agreed perfectly with the hideousness of its outward person. "A thousand, thousand blessings be upon Thee. Hallowed be Thy name! Thy kingdom come! O rapture, rapture thus to behold the golden dawn!" With which words the cat leapt upon an electric lamp and ate the bulb.

To say that I recoiled is to trifle with words. I leapt backward into a chair and cringed against the wall. The cat pursued me, shrieking Gothic praise and endearment. It put out its monstrous tongue and licked my hand. Imagine, if you can, the tongue of a cat which is twelve cats rolled into one. It was weeks before the skin-graft made necessary by this single caress was completed. But I am ahead of my story.

"No, no," I cried; "my dear animal, listen to reason. I am not your Creator. Not in the least. You owe the precious gift of life to my young friend here."

I waved my bleeding hand toward Frank. In their rapture he and Elizabeth were locked in a close embrace. That did it. Horrid, fiendish jealousy swept through the cat's whole being. All its twelve coats stood on end, the goat's eyes glared with fury, and its shovel tail lashed like that of a tiger. It sprang at Elizabeth, and with a single stroke of its powerful forepaws flung her to the ground.

I am proud to think that in that terrible moment I remembered what to do. I have always loved circuses, and I know that no trainer of tigers ever approaches his beasts without a chair in his hand. I seized up a chair and, in the approved manner, drove the monstrous creature into a corner. But what I said was not in tune with my action, or the high drama of the moment. I admit it frankly; my words were inadequate.

"You mustn't harm Miss Lavenza," I said, primly; "she is Mr. Einstein's fiancée."

But Frank's words—or rather his single word—were even more inadequate than my own. "Scat!" he shouted, kneeling by the bleeding form of his fainting beloved.

Elizabeth was to blame for programming that cat with a vocabulary culled from the Gothic Novel. "Oh, Frankenstein," it yowled, in that tremendous voice; "be not equitable to every other and trample upon me alone, to whom thy justice and even thy clemency and affection is most due. Remember that I am thy creature; I ought to be thy Adam; dub me not rather the fallen angel, whom thou drivest hence only because I love—nay reverence—thee. Jealousy of thy love makes me a fiend. Make me happy, and I shall once more be virtuous."

There is something about that kind of talk that influences everybody that hears it. I was astonished to hear Frank—who was generally contented with the utilitarian vocabulary of the scientific man—say: "Begone! I will not hear you. There can be no community between thee and me; we are enemies. Cursed be the day, abhorred devil, in which you first saw the light! You have left me no power to consider whether I am just to you or not. Begone! Relieve me of the sight of your detested form!"

Elizabeth was not the most gifted of my students, and the cat's next words lacked something of the true Gothic rhetoric. "You mean you don't love your own dear little Pussikins best," it whined. But Frank was true to the Gothic vein. "This lady is the mistress of my affections, and I acknowledge no Pussikins before her," he cried.

The cat was suddenly a picture of desolation, of rejection, of love denied. Its vocabulary moved back into high gear. "Thus I relieve thee, my creator. Thus I take from thee a sight which you abhor. Farewell!" And with one gigantic bound it leapt through the window into the quadrangle, and I heard the thunderous sound as the College gate was torn from its hinges.

I know where it went, and I felt deeply sorry for Trinity.

H. R. PERCY

THE TIMELESS ISLAND

Many tales of the mysterious or fantastic are set on islands. Perhaps strange events seem more natural in an environment cut off from our everyday world; perhaps horrors are more enjoyable if they are stranded somewhere far away; or perhaps it's just easier to create a really hair-raising atmosphere in the midst of rolling grey seas and eerie mists.

In this weird tale of a remote island, H. R. Percy paints a convincing picture of the unquiet gloom of the North Atlantic—an ex-Commander of the Royal Navy and Royal Canadian Navy, he now lives in Nova Scotia. His writings include a novel, Flotsam, *and a biography,* Joseph Howe, *as well as the collection* The Timeless Island and Other Stories.

JOAN and Edgar scrambled ashore under the disapproving eye of the skipper, a little man with an aggressively poised chin and a forbidding cast to his eye. He had made it clear that he did not make a practice of carrying mere sightseers in his boat, and had hinted in a sinister manner that if they were not ready to step aboard when he called on his return trip, he would find great satisfaction in leaving them on the island for three days.

The boat swung away almost before they were clear, and made off round the headland with a derisive hoot. They were left with a sudden sense of loneliness amid immensity. The lapping of the sea seemed only to emphasize a silence into which their footfalls on the planks broke with disconcerting echoes. A flock of gulls rose from the rocks in raucous protest, and settled uneasily at a distance as these alien creatures invaded their peace.

Edgar looked about him, still misty-eyed with remembering, at widely scattered crofts and the tiny isolated kirk set like a watch-tower on the shoulder of the hill.

"That's the site of the old camp up there," he said, pointing. "Not much sign of it now. Care to have a look?"

"All right." Even Joan's tact could not instil enthusiasm into her acquiescence. She had begun to suspect that Edgar's urge to revisit Dunkelvie arose from no more than a nostalgic impulse. The preposterous thought even crossed her mind that the whole concept of their tour, planned and improved upon through the long Ontario winter, had been founded upon a secret yearning of Edgar's to come back here. He was capable of that. A place like this would appeal to his imagination; the wide expanses, the restful contours, the sunlit sweeps of heather, and the soothing sense of a host of tomorrows waiting to be lived without haste or calculation. Of friends, it was sufficient that they lived and were in accord with one, but familiar places tugged relentlessly, dangling promises of resurrected experience. She had not been married to Edgar for a year without discovering his profound sentimentality, and learning to make allowances for it. All the same, an army camp was hardly a place to yearn for, much less to make a pilgrimage to.

Of course, there would have been comrades, but Edgar could surely have re-established contact with them, had he cared. A woman, perhaps? She thrust the thought impatiently aside and bent to pick a spray of flowers growing at the side of the path. This was no day, and she was in no mood, for a conducted tour. She felt girlish and inconsequent. For her there was sufficient pleasure to be found in wandering and gathering flowers, and letting the spirit of the place seep into her.

If Edgar once persuaded himself that she was interested, he would be devastatingly eloquent.

"I suppose you are wondering why I wanted to come back here?"

She looked up. So there was a story! Despite his nonchalance he was obviously agog with it. She could sense it surging up within him in response to the influence of the place.

"It did cross my mind," she said.

"It's not an easy thing to explain, even to myself." His eyes ranged the island thoughtfully. "Certain things happened here which I didn't question very deeply at the time. Things perhaps better forgotten. But I couldn't forget. I tried to think the thing out, but in Kitchener it all seemed so irrational. And the more I puzzled over it, the more I wanted to come back here, to convince myself that my imagination had not been running away with me.

"You know, Joan, this is not quite the Dunkelvie I remember." The softly spoken words seemed to dissolve in the silence about them. Joan showed surprise.

"Oh, topographically it's the same. The crofts are the same as they've been for centuries, and no doubt the people are, too. Left alone, they would carry on their way of life to the end of time; life is the only gauge they have of time.

"You can have no idea what this place is like in winter. The greyness of it, and the perpetual damp. No wonder the crofters built their houses with walls like fortresses; the damp used to eat its way into those huts of ours as if they had been made of blotting paper. The mist would close about us without warning, billowing in from the sea like the smoke of some colossal fire, and it would hang about for days, as though it couldn't shake itself free of the spiky heather stalks. Then a wind would spring up, and it would be so cold that we wished the mist back again. The rain came on those winds like icy claws tearing at your face."

They had turned aside from the path and were approaching a broad expanse of blooming heather, sloping gently up and presenting a purple shoulder to the sky. Joan exclaimed at the beauty of it.

"Here," said Edgar, putting the full irony of it into his tone, "is where the camp stood."

"But there's nothing left," Joan said. "Did they pull it down?"

"I really don't know, but if the army didn't, either the islanders or the elements would. The people of Dunkelvie would have been only too pleased when the wind carried away the last trace of our occupation."

"Why?"

"I suppose it was an instinctive dislike. If you tackled them about it, no doubt they would give you a lengthy catalogue of our sins—tell you that we played heathen music on the sabbath, and played at cards, and whistled after their daughters, and generally stood host to the Devil—but it went deeper than that, much deeper."

As they walked, both were searching for some evidence, some trifling memorial of a phase in Edgar's life, but they found none.

"You know well enough, Joan," he said, turning to look into her eyes, "that I'm not one to get bored easily. Give me a book and I could be happy in prison, yet during that winter here there were times when I found myself making the most morbid speculations about the purpose of life. All the books had been so thoroughly read and talked over that we knew their characters as well as we knew each other, and they got on our nerves to about the same degree.

"You can imagine, then, how welcome McCleod was. It was in that period of ultra-boredom following the somewhat forced excitement of Christmas and New Year. I was gazing idly out of the mess window when McCleod was cast up, as it were, out of the sea, and stood shivering on the jetty. Even against the immensity of the sea he looked vast: it reminded me of a picture I once saw of Gulliver surveying the shores of Lilliput.

"I went down to meet him. He stood there looking about him, and as I drew near I could hear that he was humming one of those mournful Scottish airs—the kind that always seems to me to be full of disquieting associations.

"My voice startled him. His eyes were wild, in that moment, as if the words had come out of the air. He looked around him quickly and fixed me at last with a look of relief.

"Come to join us?" I asked him again. He said yes, he had (with a pardonable lack of enthusiasm), and introduced himself in a rich highland accent as James Cameron McCleod. As we walked back to the camp he kept gazing from croft to croft in that strange preoccupied way of his, and I found it difficult to get a word out of him.

"He was a fine-looking fellow. You could imagine him standing on a rock and brandishing a claymore in the face of an advancing army. But a very brief acquaintance was sufficient to dispel that illusion. He was too sensitive to be heroic in that way. I'm not suggesting that he was a coward. Courage was a quality very little in demand in our situation, but I would say from the way in which McCleod faced up to the rigours of Dunkelvie that if he had courage, it was of the passive sort. His was the spirit of martyrdom rather than of rebellion."

On Joan's suggestion they spread Edgar's raincoat on the heather and sat down to eat the sandwiches she had brought. For a time Edgar's narrative was punctuated by rustlings of paper and periods of silent application.

"It's always struck me as queer that McCleod and I should have got on so well together." Edgar pondered it during the mastication of a whole sandwich.

"You see, perhaps the secret was in my readiness to take him seriously. I think Mac's difficulty was that he wanted desperately to appear normal, but at the same time there was another side of his nature that demanded expression. A sort of mysticism, I suppose you'd call it.

"You can imagine how the average soldier would shy away from that sort of thing.

"For the first week or so he was popular enough, but when the novelty wore off and he began to corner the guys one by one and quote outlandish poetry, and sound their opinions on matters like spiritualism and reincarnation, they dropped him as if he'd been a leper."

He reached for another sandwich and studied it with profound concentration. Joan watched him closely, held by the sincerity of his manner. He spoke as if her reception of the story was a matter of vital importance.

"He interested me. It was obvious that he was no crank, and it seemed illogical that an intelligent man should pursue such morbid interests.

"I suppose it was my curiosity, coupled with my readiness to take him seriously, that drew him to me. And as I got to know him it became apparent there was something on his mind.

"We were alone in the mess one Sunday afternoon. The others had been driven to their beds by sheer boredom. I rather fancied myself as a painter in those days, and I decided to take advantage of the quiet to put the finishing touches to a still life I had been striving to master for several weeks. McCleod stood behind me and watched, making an occasional comment. Just by way of conversation I asked him what he thought of Dunkelvie.

"He took it up almost eagerly. 'You know,' he said, strolling across to the window (he had a habit of conversing with his back to the listener), 'you know, there's something queer about this place. Something I don't understand.'

"I said nothing. After all, we all felt that way about it. But he went on to tell me that Dunkelvie was as familiar to him as if he had lived there for years. 'As soon as I saw it on the horizon I knew it; recognized its shape,' he said. 'Couldna take my eyes off it. I knew exactly what to expect as we came round the point; the crofts, the kirk, the very rocks on the shore.'

"I suggested that perhaps he had seen a picture of it somewhere, but he waved the idea aside impatiently."

Edgar leaned back on his elbow and gazed up into Joan's eyes with profound earnestness, anxious, it seemed, to impress upon her the importance of all this.

"What he said was: 'I think I've lived before.'

"I straightened up. McCleod's back was still squarely turned, and he stood there with a forced nonchalance as if disowning so preposterous a statement. I returned to my work and said nothing; but the words had thrown between us a curtain of embarrassment which kept us silent the whole afternoon.

"He began to show an interest in painting, and more for the sake of the distraction than from the hope of worthwhile results, I gave him a few simple lessons. The brush in his great fur-backed hand seemed to have no more artistic potentiality than a skewer through a joint of beef. Yet he made surprisingly rapid progress.

"It wasn't long before I realized that he had the makings of a real painter, and the urge was obviously so strong within him that eventually I withdrew quietly into the background and left him to it. There was nothing further I could teach him, and he was making better use of the canvas than I could ever hope to do.

"In February, after a frost or two, we enjoyed a brief, premature spring. Mac took to painting in the open. His work was purely experimental, and he usually came back morose and frowning, complaining of his inability to get down on canvas what was in his mind, as if that was a curse peculiar to him.

"His pictures lacked something vital—conviction, inspiration, what you will. And the repeated frustration seemed to prey upon him, darkening his countenance and his mind.

"I saw him often standing inert and pensive before the easel. Sometimes I passed quite close—close enough to inspect a blank or a defaced canvas—and he never spared me a glance. The others saw him too, and twitted him with seeking inspiration; but I had already begun to suspect that he was chasing phantoms.

"Then one afternoon I saw him from a distance, working with fervent, almost passionate concentration. He jabbed at the palette as if he begrudged the time spent in replenishing his brush. His easel—a crude affair knocked up out of packing cases—was set up in a hollow between two of the guns. Down there."

Edgar pointed down the seaward slope, and Joan, following the line of his arm, saw a shallow depression with one side dropping sheer to the sea.

"Just about where you see that puddle shining in the sun. I say, that's queer! Water lying on the peat, like that. I wonder if——" The speculation was never uttered. Edgar stood up abruptly and brushed a crumb or two from his jacket. While Joan packed away the debris of their meal he lit his pipe and stood smoking thoughtfully.

"I couldn't imagine why he should choose such a spot. There is a view of the sea, it's true, but it's by no means the best view. As I watched, however, I noticed that his eyes never left the canvas.

"When I came that way three hours later he was still painting frenziedly, regardless of the passing of time and the chilling dampness of the air. It was the failing light that eventually broke through his preoccupation. He returned to the mess looking pale, empty-eyed, and emotionally exhausted.

"For several days all his leisure was passed at that spot, sometimes painting feverishly, sometimes in a sort of coma. If you spoke to him he would start as if awakened from sleep.

"The fruit of McCleod's brief afflatus was the portrait of a young woman. Perhaps in the niceties of execution it fell short of his earlier efforts, but for sheer vitality and boldness I have seldom seen it equalled.

"Yet there was something undefined about it. It was at the

same time vivid and vague, like a dream, or a reflection in water not quite still. There were unexpected lights and shadows, unlooked-for vagaries of colour, which somehow combined to unsettle me.

"The subject of the picture was handsome enough, with very dark, appealing eyes and fine waist-long tresses cascading about her shoulders. But I would not have lived with that picture for the world. I could not have been in the same room without being aware all the time of its soft, imploring gaze following me with a sort of spectral intensity. The background was of frigid green — a mere limbo — so that the face appeared to float just beneath the surface of an icy pool. The chill seemed to communicate itself to the atmosphere, and I felt it creeping into my very bones.

"I turned away from it with a shudder and went to the fire where Mac sat shivering, casting an immense, Buddha-like shadow. He got up hastily, put away the picture, and came back to expose himself greedily to the flames.

"'It's a masterpiece,' I said, 'no doubt of that.'

"He continued to gaze into the fire without comment, seeming neither glad of my praise nor skeptical of it. He looked limp, played out. 'What I can't understand,' I said, 'is what made you do it.'

"His brow glistened in the firelight, and his hands were clenched tight. How plainly I can see him crouching there, with that great shadow hovering behind as if it gloated over him.

"'I couldn't help myself,' he told me. 'It's not really my picture at all. I only painted what I saw. And once I began, I couldn't stop.'

"Although his fingers were stiff, and his arm ached, and he was frozen to the bone, he had to go on. When it was all over, he said, it was like starting from a doze; and there was the picture — a tantalizing fragment of a forgotten dream.

"But who was she? I wanted to know. I was half-prepared for his reply, but the look by which it was accompanied appalled me.

"'Ah! Who is she? I'd give anything in the world to know,'

he said. 'Anything. She's out of the past. Out of an earlier life.'

"What, he kept saying, had she to do with him? If only he could remember! But always it just eluded him."

They walked on in silence for some time. Joan, with the sun warm upon her cheek, emerged for a moment from the mesmeric chill into which Edgar's words and her own imagination had plunged her, and darted aside to add to her nosegay.

It was another change in his tone that brought her to heel.

"About that time there was a period of intense activity. The camp shook off its winter lethargy and began preparations for the visit of a Cabinet Minister, who was touring the outposts of defence. Night and day aircraft tested our alertness, and the island shook under our practice fire. Hour after hour during those chilly nights our searchlights scoured the darkness. And it rained incessantly until the peaty soil yielded to the tread like a sodden sponge.

"It was towards the end of one of those night exercises. I was making a last tour of the sites, following roughly the line we are following now. The searchlights had gone out, and the beam of my flashlight cut through the slanting rain and struck a glistening oval before me on the wet, quaggy heather. The rain pattered on my cape incessantly with a rhythm that had a lulling effect on my mind."

He stopped by the pool they had seen from higher up the slope. There was an odd suggestion of solemnity in his pose.

"I was midway between the last two guns—somewhere here—when I saw it. A white object thrusting up out of the heather. Something shockingly familiar in outline. Something alien and awful at such a time and place. I bent closer to look.

"It was—" he glanced quickly at Joan with mingling relish and apology. "It was a human hand. A woman's hand, I judged, held aloft aimlessly; and around it in all directions the heather grew even and undisturbed as a carpet."

"Edgar!" Joan had no clear idea what the exclamation was intended to convey, but something of her inward shudder went into it, and she saw it register on Edgar's pensive face.

"Whatever did you do?" she asked quickly.

"I shouted to raise the alarm. While I stood here listening to the voices approaching through the darkness, the implications of my discovery began to crowd upon me. The hand implied a body, and a body in such a place implied murder. But who? By whom?

"The tide of activity swept over me," he went on. "They came with spades and planks and set to with a great deal of chatter. McCleod came and stood beside me, gripping my arm painfully as he watched the exhumation. As it grew lighter I could see that his face was haggard and grey.

"By the time the diggers had finished their work it was almost daylight. They lifted out a pallid shape, flecked brown with peat, and lowered it onto the heather.

"Where the rain had washed it clean, the body showed not a blemish, not a scar. It was like a sculpture in fine ivory, graceful and—and sublime.

"'Anyone know who she is?' I remember someone asking. Mac stirred beside me, but said nothing. His eyes were fixed on the still face of the girl with a strange, questioning look; and when I looked in the same direction a cold thrill of recognition passed through me. The same face, the same hair, damp and disordered now; the same disquieting pallor, and something of that same suggestion of unreality.

"Then I remembered him standing there painting, on that very spot. 'I only painted in what I saw,' he had said. And I remembered the look of torment on his face the day he finished the picture. He had been extremely preoccupied ever since that day. His behaviour alone would have been sufficient, when cool heads began to consider, to lay him open to suspicion.

"But there was an unexpected development.

"Naturally, every effort was made to establish the identity of the girl. Visits were made to all the crofts and a sort of census taken of the population. The crofters were of little practical help, but they all dropped hints of a knowledge they did not care to share with us. One or two of them did unbend, though, so far as to say that she was a suicide who had been refused burial in the kirkyard.

"Their confounded indifference blocked our inquiries more effectively than downright lying could have done, and I doubt if the startling fact which transformed the whole affair would ever have come to light if it hadn't been for McCleod's obsession.

"During our house-to-house check-up, it had fallen to Mac to visit a lonely croft on the remote side of the island. We shall shortly come in sight of it. It was managed by an ancient crone and her half-witted son.

"He told me he had never been more certain of anything in his life, than that he had been in that house before. He didn't glean much from that first interview, but something convinced him that there, if anywhere, the solution to the mystery lay, and he resolved to go back and get to the bottom of it."

Edgar, as they came at that moment round a large, naked outcrop, pointed ahead, where the cottage of which he spoke rose in squat silhouette. Above it a thread of peat smoke climbed into the sultry sky.

"There it is. I wonder who keeps it now. The old woman would be dead by this time, of course, and I can't imagine the son running the place alone.

"They were a queer pair. McCleod took me with him when he went again. In the meantime the body had been reburied, and we all shared in the fervent hope that we had seen and heard the last of it. All, that is, except McCleod. He was as anxious to solve the puzzle as we were to forget it.

"Well, he managed to talk me into coming to this croft with him, although it was a damp and bitterly cold night. He was carrying a package which I had little difficulty in identifying as that creepy picture of his, with which he hoped to surprise the old girl into talking.

"You can see that the door is pretty solid. Mac announced our arrival by a lusty kick with his army-size twelve. The door opened a few degrees with uncanny silence and from the crack a face peered out—the most puckered face I have ever seen. A pair of faded eyes looked us over cynically. I heard Mac's boots scraping uneasily on the patch of shingle before the door."

They were now quite close to the cottage.

"To my surprise," Edgar went on, "the crone opened the door wide and shuffled into the gloom beyond. We hesitated for a moment and then followed her in. McCleod ducked low and literally filled the doorway with his great bulk. The woman disposed herself with painful care on a crude, high-backed chair. She pointed across the hearth to a long chest, polished black by generations of uneasy sitters. We sat down like a couple of penitent children, and waited.

"The room was lit only by a small lamp with a blackened glass, and the red glow of the peats. It was very small, yet even coming in from the total darkness I found it difficult to distinguish all the objects in it. The old woman's son sat on a stool in the darkest corner, watching with eyes that glowed out at us like an animal's.

"Most of the floor space was taken up by a scrubbed table and a bed. I suppose the walls had once been whitewashed, but they were now slate-grey, and in the region of the hearth almost black. Overhead was a dark cavity crossed by rafters on which hung the provisions and utensils of the household.

"The silence of those first few minutes had a stifled quality about it. Afterwards I put it down to the fact that there wasn't a clock in the place, but at the time it was eerie enough.

"Mac began to stammer out an apology for our intrusion, but she cut him short by saying she'd expected us, or she'd have been abed hours ago. 'Ye've come about Maggie,' she said.

"'Is Maggie the name of the girl we found buried in the peat?' I asked. I was anxious to get it over and get away from the place. She said, rather curtly, that she knew of only one being buried loose in Dunkelvie.

"McCleod began to unwrap his parcel.

"She interlaced her fleshless fingers and swayed in her chair. When Mac held up the picture so that the glow of the peat fell on it, she studied it closely.

"'I mind they used to say the quean was pretty and black-eyed; and my mother used to weep when she combed my bonnie black hair, and say it was just like poor Maggie's.' There was a tear in her own eye as she pointed at the long tresses in the picture. She took off her starched cap, and I saw with an eerie shock that she was quite bald.

"'Maggie was my mother's sister.' She paused, as if remembering something. 'He painted Maggie's picture, too,' she said. She stood up and shuffled across the room, holding up the lamp to throw light on a picture on the wall. We went to look. The canvas was dark with age, and its subject was barely distinguishable, but beneath the grime I thought I saw a more conventional version of McCleod's picture. McCleod said 'Ah!'

"Maggie, the old woman went on to tell us, was the bonniest lass in Dunkelvie. She was always blithe as the sun, and there wasn't a young man on the island but wished to marry her. But she showed no favour.

"Eventually it was a sailor-laddie from the mainland who won Maggie's heart. 'Frae then on,' the old woman said, 'her smile was for him alone.' She would wait and wish all week long for his coming, and when the boat came she would run down the bank and wait at the waterside for her lover. They would walk together along the shore until the sun was down and sometimes he would make drawings of her. At night in bed Maggie would tell her sister of her great love, and sigh for the day when she should be married.

"At that point the hag jabbed a finger at the picture and said in a shaky voice: 'Such eyes were made for weeping. Such a tender heart was made for sorrow.'

"The young man went away on a long voyage. Maggie implored her father to let them be married before he went, but he would hear nothing of it. Time enough to think of that, he said, when the voyage was over. It would prove whether her lover was true or no.

"Maggie said no more, but she cried all night on her sister's shoulder. She became pale and dull, and was like a cloud about the house. One night the old woman's mother found Maggie distracted with grief. She said she was no more than a shameless wench, and not fit to share a bed with a pure, innocent lassie. Her sister managed at last to soothe her to sleep.

"But the next morning Maggie was gone, and that same evening they recovered her body from the sea and brought her to the house."

Joan and Edgar had now circled the cottage and were heading back the way they had come. The barking of a dog died away behind them, leaving a double weight of silence, into which Edgar's voice broke again with a suggestion of effort.

"As if the loss of Maggie wasn't trouble enough for the family, all the inhabitants were against allowing her burial in the kirkyard. Maggie's father never recovered from the humiliation, and died soon after.

"I can see that old woman now, sitting there with her eyes fixed in a watery stare. Her little red pointed tongue kept flickering out over her shapeless lips. She seemed to have forgotten us.

"'Poor Maggie was buried in the heather abune the bay, where she used to bide for her laddie,' she said, in a thin unsteady voice. 'But she waited long in her cauld bed, and nae lover came. Every Sabbath e'en my mother used to walk that way an' say a bit prayer for her sister buried there on the lonely moor. She feared the lass couldnae rest in unhallowed ground.'

"She turned up her eyes to the rafters, and her lips formed soundless words. Neither she nor her son stirred as we got up and went out into the night.

"The full impact of it didn't strike me till we got outside. In that small, smoky cottage, the youth of the old woman's mother had seemed a thing of yesterday. You could almost hear the echoes of the loud voice of Maggie's father forbidding her marriage, and the whispers of the two girls as they lay together in the darkness—perhaps in that very bed I saw.

"But as we walked back to the camp, the thought which had lain somewhere deep down in my mind—kept down by the sense of timelessness that prevailed in the place—suddenly asserted its shocking logic.

"That old woman was ninety years old if she was a day, and the tragedy of Maggie had taken place before she was born—before her mother was married. What we were asked to believe

— what we were forced to believe eventually — was that the girl's body had been lying there a hundred years or more."

"But honey," Joan said to him — there could be no doubt of his seriousness, "that's not possible."

Edgar turned upon her. "Oh, but it is. The CO followed the matter up, and apparently it's been known before. Bodies have been preserved in the peat indefinitely, and that one might have lain there another century, if the tremors caused by our guns had not coincided with that long spell of rain and brought it to the surface."

"And that, I suppose," said Joan, not without relief, "is the end of the story?"

"It ought to have been. I think that in time Mac would have shaken off his obsession, or at least have kept it under until he left the island. It was obvious to everyone that he was mentally and morally ill. I had the thing out with him once.

"'Do you really believe the body has been lying there all these years, preserved in the peat,' I asked him. 'If you insist on reducing it to a mere matter of chemistry, yes,' he said.

"'And the alternative?' I prompted him. He flashed me a look of acute misery and repeated the old woman's words. 'She waited lang in her cauld bed, but nae lover came.'

"'So?' I said.

"'So there she must lie until her lover returns.'

"'What nonsense,' I said, unable to suppress my skepticism. McCleod looked shocked and hurt, and walked away. That just about ended our intimacy.

"As I said, I think he would have recovered in time if— But about two weeks later it was reported that the hand had appeared once more, rising out of the heather as if it grew there.

"The CO began negotiations with the natives to have the body transferred to the kirkyard, but they wouldn't hear of it. They were as bitterly opposed to the idea as their grandfathers had been, and in the end the Major had to admit defeat. He had the body exhumed and buried deeper.

"But in less than a month it broke surface again, and men far less fanciful than McCleod began to express unorthodox opinions. Mac haunted the spot continually. He no longer confided in me, but I watched him pretty closely, and I could see that he was at breaking point.

"I saw the terror in his eyes when it was announced that half a ton of concrete was to be dumped over the burial place next morning.

"But I think it was the prank played by some of the less discerning of our messmates that broke McCleod. The boredom and the continuous foul weather tended to distort their sense of humour. For sanity's sake they had to get a laugh out of the affair, and Mac, with his mystical obsession, was the obvious butt. A deep grave had been dug, and the body wrapped in a blanket, left in an empty hut, in readiness for the morning.

"You may well imagine that the girl furnished just about the only topic of conversation that evening. It played on all our nerves a little, and most of us drank more than we were accustomed to.

"Some of the fellows grew indignant and pretty loud about the attitude of the islanders, and when they got up and went out I was fully convinced they were going to make trouble.

"Well, they were, but it wasn't the sort of trouble I expected. About a quarter of an hour later they staggered back into the mess with something wrapped in a blanket. There was a stunned silence, and one of them said in a tipsy voice: 'I say, you guys, we've brought the lady in for a drink. Show her we're gen'lemen, not like them other hypocrites.'"

Eyes wide with horror, Joan drew away with a cry.

"How horrible. Oh, Edgar, how could you!"

"Steady old girl. I assure you I had nothing to do with it. Of course it may not have been the body at all. I doubt if it was. After all they weren't so very drunk, and they were a decent crowd really."

"Didn't you ever find out then?" she asked. She fancied that there was a barely perceptible hesitation before he said: "No, I never found out."

"Then what happened?"

"Well, Mac had been sitting in the corner alone. His hair

was all over the place and his eyes had a fixed, glassy look. He looked pretty far gone. When the boys barged in with—with the thing—the blanket, he just about went mad. It took six of us to hold him while we bundled those fools out of the door.

"That broke the evening up, and when the uproar died down—and there was an infernal row, I can tell you—we all went to our beds.

"The next morning McCleod was missing. We never saw him again. There was a large-scale search, and an exhaustive inquiry, both of which yielded nothing."

They walked in silence till they came once more to the tiny pool. Joan was searching in her mind for a possible explanation of it all, and a possible end. As they paused by the glistening water she said: "What do you think happened to him?"

Edgar said in a voice slightly hushed: "Well, it did occur to me that the party searching the island for McCleod, and the other mixing concrete and dumping it here, may possibly—just possibly—have been working at cross purposes."

"How dreadful," she said, as his meaning came to her. "And yet—" she took a pace nearer, casting a shadow across the pool, "—and yet how right."

"If the concrete hadn't sunk and become water-logged, we might perhaps still see the cross I marked on it before it hardened, and the letters RIP, which in this instance seemed to have more than their usual significance. It was——"

He was interrupted by the distant hoot of the boat's siren. Remembering the skipper's implied threat, they both glanced incredulously at their watches.

"It can't be as late as that!"

"I told you time had its own rules on Dunkelvie."

They joined hands and ran for it. The flowers Joan had carried in her hand during their long walk scattered slowly over the surface of the pool where she had dropped them; and the pool looked serene and beautiful in the sun, though there was none to see.

HUGH GARNER

THE PREMEDITATED DEATH OF SAMUEL GLOVER

One of the most interesting—and dismaying—theories of human existence is that of predestination: the belief that every detail of our lives is preordained, that accidents do not *happen, that free will is an illusion. In this next story, Hugh Garner (1913-1979) raises some intriguing questions on the subject. The tale makes good use of the workaday world so vividly evoked in Garner's realistic novels, like* Cabbagetown *and* A Nice Place to Visit, *and his short stories, as well as in the series of detective novels about Inspector Walter McDumont of the Toronto Police Department that Garner was working on when he died.*

Hugh Garner's Best Stories *won a Governor General's Award in 1963.*

IT'S been nothing but questions all day at the office. Every few minutes one of the other draftsmen would come over to my board and ask me about Sam's death. "What happened last night? Were you with him? Did it knock him down? Run over him? How'd he look? Was there much blood?"

They have no idea what it's like seeing a friend get killed like that, and having to answer all the questions by the police, the taxi company lawyer, and then by the fellows at work the next day. I'm going to tell it once more, the whole thing, and then I'm through.

Every night at five o'clock for the last seven or eight years Sam Glover and I have taken the elevator together, going home. Sam would buy his evening paper in the lobby, and then we'd walk up the street as far as Queen where we separated, Sam to take a westbound streetcar, and me to take one going east.

It got to be a habit, this three-block walk, and I enjoyed it because Sam was an interesting old fellow to talk to. He was a bachelor who lived with a married sister away out in the west end of town. From some of the things he told me on these short walks I learned that he was a believer in things like fate and premeditation. It was his favourite subject, and sometimes he'd point to people who passed us on the street and say, "There goes a man hurrying to his fate," or "He wants to reach his rendezvous, that one."

When I'd laugh, he'd say, "You'll find out some day that it's no joke. I've seen it happen. Every man is predestined to meet his death at a time and place already chosen, my boy."

I'd laugh and shake my head.

It was about three years ago that Sam told me where he was going to die. We were waiting for the lights to change at the intersection of Adelaide Street, when Sam said, "This is the place where fate is going to catch up to me."

I looked down at him and laughed, thinking he was joking. He was the type of mousy little guy who would joke like that—or dismember a corpse.

"You may laugh, son, but it's true," he asserted in the good-natured, yet serious, way he had.

"Do you mean to tell me that you're going to be killed on this corner?" I asked.

"That's right," he answered soberly.

When the lights changed, we crossed the street. I said to Sam, "If you know that you're going to be killed here, why do you take this way home? You could walk a block east or west and take the streetcar from there."

"It wouldn't be much use trying to avoid it," he answered. "Some day I'd forget, or have some business to transact down here——"

"Well, suppose you decided not to die at all. You could move to another town and live for ever."

"Nobody lives for ever," he answered patiently. "You can't avoid your fate. This is where it will happen, and nothing I can do will prevent it. I'm just hoping that it won't be for some time yet." He looked up at me and smiled apologetically, but I could see that he meant every word.

After that I brought the subject up occasionally as we were crossing Adelaide Street, kidding him about being short-sighted, and about getting killed before his time if he wasn't careful. He would only smile at me and say, "You wait and see."

Last night we left the office as usual, about two minutes to five, in order to beat the rush to the elevators. Sam bought his paper in the lobby, and we went out into the street.

As we brushed through the five-o'clock crowd I asked Sam how his dyke drawings for the Mountview Refinery were coming along, and he told me he expected to finish them in a week; he was only waiting for some new tank specifications from McGuire, one of the engineers.

Looking up into the blue sky above the buildings I said, "It's going to be a nice evening. A change from the rain we've been having."

"Yes, it is. I'm going to do a little lawn bowling tonight," he answered. "It'll be my first chance this year. The greens have been a mess up to now."

When we reached the corner of Adelaide the lights were in our favour and we began to cross with the crowd. They changed from green to amber when we were half-way across, but we still had plenty of time. He stuck close to me as he always did. I saw this taxi cut around the traffic and begin to cross the intersection as soon as it got the green light, so I shouted to Sam and ran the last few yards to the sidewalk.

I looked around and saw the taxi pick him up and throw him with a sickening plop against a hydrant about twenty feet from the corner. There was the scream of the taxi's brakes and a lot of yelling from the crowd.

By the time I got there two men had laid Sam out on the sidewalk. Everybody was crowding around to get a better look at him. He was dead, of course. One side of his head was squashed like the soft spot in an orange.

A policeman butted his way through the crowd and asked what had happened. The hack driver came over from his car and told the policeman that he hadn't had a chance, this old man ran right in front of his cab. He seemed to be a nice young fellow, and he wanted us all to believe him. I told the policeman I was a friend of Sam's, and that I'd seen the accident. I assured the driver that it wasn't his fault.

The taxi company lawyer came to my place later in the evening and questioned me about the accident. "I can't understand why he'd turn around and run the other way," he kept on saying.

"I've told you it wasn't your driver's fault, so why do you keep asking me questions like that?"

"O.K. I'm only trying to work this thing out in case they have an inquest," he said.

If they have an inquest, I'm going to tell the truth. I've been thinking it over and I feel sure that Sam would have wanted it that way.

I had nothing against the old fellow, but after listening for so long to him bragging about knowing where he was going to die, it seemed I had to find out whether he was right or not. When I shouted at him to turn back, it wasn't me talking at all. Call it fate or predestination, or what you like, but that's what killed Sam Glover.

Y V E S   T H E R I A U L T

THE BARREN FIELD

Extreme situations have always played an important role in the fiction of Yves Thériault, Quebec's celebrated story-teller. Many of his stories—like the piece included here—have an element of fantasy. Thériault is of French and Montagnais descent. He left school when he was fifteen and, after various jobs, became a writer for the National Film Board and then for Radio-Canada. His output is astonishing—he has written over 1,300 radio and television scripts, and some fifty books, including a series of thrilling novels set in the north, some of which are about the Montagnais (Labrador Indians). Thériault wrote "The Barren Field" in English, but most of his work is in French. Four novels that have been translated into English are Agaguk, Ashini, N'Tsuk, *and* Agoak.

"Cette année-ci, le blé sera beau car la terre a bu le sang de l'homme."

(This year, the wheat will be beautiful because the earth has drunk the blood of man.)

(Calloc'h)

FOR thirty days, Christina Sorensen spread her arms out and stood above the barren field that was all the land she owned, and she let the setting sun throw her shadow on the parched yellow soil. She was a tall bony woman, built like a man. Her shadow was enormous on the field, and because of the outstretched arms it was in the shape of a cross.

She moved this way and that, throwing the shadow over the whole field, the bare half-acre she had fenced with iron posts and good strong wire. And as she moved she muttered the only prayer of faith she knew.

"God will make the wheat grow," she repeated endlessly, "since the soil will not." After two weeks she knew the work had been useless and the nightly prayer became a gesture. A concession to the people in the valley, watching her toiling up here; watching her because they feared the enormous woman who threw rocks at them if they came up the path to her cabin.

There remained no alternative for Christina. The words of the old songs and the sayings of the story-tellers, that she had learned as a child in the land across the sea, were now all that was left to her. Did they not tell the secret of the growing wheat? But no one could say Christina had not tried the way of God first.

It had taken a year after Big Bill Sorensen's death to make up her mind about the barren field and the wheat she wanted to grow in it.

She had walked into Mort's store one day, her face grimy with the labour of fence-building, and she had said, "I want seed wheat, Mort."

The storekeeper looked at her strangely, but he went to get the wheat.

He set the bag against the wall next to the front door and

walked slowly back to his stool behind the counter. Outside was the maddening glare and the visible heat-waves, but the long, low store was cool and restful. It was littered with the goods of desert living, the barrels of lard, the sacks of feed, the bunches of spurs-straps or rein leather hanging from the rafters. Galvanized pails and cheap stetsons piled on the counter, and a row of high boots standing on a shelf near the ceiling. Mort pushed the stool aside and leaned against the shelving. He slowly rolled himself a cigarette, not touching the money Christina Sorensen had laid on the counter.

"Did you buy land, Christina?" he asked. "Did you buy land in the valley?"

She shook her head. "No . . . I'm sowing wheat in my field up there."

Mort Stevenson shrugged his shoulders and looked at Christina a long time. But the big, brawny woman with the wide hands met Mort's eyes steadily, as he searched for a meaning to the seed wheat.

"It's your land, Christina."

"Yes," she said, and she walked to the bag of wheat, lightly picked up the hundred pounds in one flip of the wrist, and went out the door.

Mort stood by the window watching her ride away on the big gelding, her long powerful legs dangling grotesquely on each side of the horse.

Through the dusty panes, he stared at her thoughtfully as she nudged the horse up the winding path full in the blaze of the afternoon sun. She was climbing steadily towards the cabin perched precariously on the ledge, a thousand feet up. The cabin and the half-acre field below it were all Big Bill had left her when he died.

From the ledge, the small field came down abruptly, yielding to the slope, a neatly defined square in the jagged face of the mountain. The valley was a long narrow crevice between the high peaks. When the first gold-hungry men came to the valley, they built the town at the dry end, where the gold was. They dug deep-reaching wells for the elusive water, and named the town after Baldy Connor, who struck water on the twentieth day, and after the wells, because they saved them from death, since they did not know of the river that flowed thirty miles away. Farmers eventually found the river, and grew seeds and raised cattle, but that was later, and the men of Connor's Wells did not know about them either for quite a while. Here, around the town and under it, the soil was yellow, implacable, refusing to feed anything but mesquite trees. As the flat valley bottom surged suddenly into a stiff slope, a hundred feet from the town's last house, reaching for the high peaks of the Mother Mountains, the dry yellow earth became granite, still more implacable, and the paths were hewn by wind and rain or the hoofs of weary horses across the face of the gigantic range.

The only soil there was on the mountain was the plot of land staked by Big Bill Sorensen as a living-place, when he came from the east with the early settlers. A pocket of the useless earth hanging on the hill, clearly seen from the town below. Near in measured distance, but very far because of the tortuous path that climbed to it, retraced its steps to find better footing, then circled around boulders, to climb some more before retracing again. A slippery, treacherous road, nearly impassable to any but Christina Sorensen and the mule-footed gelding.

Often, Big Bill had spoken of the day when he would hoe the ground, and fertilize it, and bring water from some mountain spring he was going to find, so the seeds would grow. And as he talked of that, Christina would smile, and nestle closer to the lumbering giant, because she loved the seeds and the plowed fields, and the wheat that reminded her of the land where she was born. But Big Bill never got around to plowing the earth, or fertilizing it. He was looking for the gold he never found.

And often, as often as Big Bill had spoken of the wheat he was to grow, Christina had thought of the secret she knew that would bring up the seeds in the barren earth, that would save looking for improbable water, but had never told Bill what the secret was, because Bill was dreaming, and he would not listen to her, only to his dream. So she would become silent after a while, and dream with him.

For days after she had come to buy the seed wheat, Mort watched her toiling up there in the field, carrying stones by hand, stacking them in a neat pile in the middle of the enclosure. She pulled out the mesquite and hoed the ground. Foot by sweating foot, using a hand hoe, she broke up the hard-packed earth that had been baked by the relentless sun for centuries.

As she bent and pushed the hoe into the ground, as she straightened to survey the work done and that which was left to do, Mort knew her great body was covered with sweat under the long skirt and the rough cloth bodice.

She turned the ground, shook out every stone that was in it; when the earth was ready, she sowed the wheat.

That first night, she stood over the field as the moon came up, and in a great raucous voice that tumbled down into the valley, and that was heard inside the houses where the frightened people listened, she sang a strange chant of her youth, of the far-away country whence she had come, only a girl, to marry Big Bill Sorensen who searched for gold in the Barren Hills of the great south-west.

The sound reaching Connor's Wells in the quiet night was like the howl of a wounded animal. Only the wheat seed and the God of the Mountains knew that the strange music and the foreign words asked for the kindness of the long-abandoned soil to the seed it now held.

But the second night, and every night for thirty days after that, Christina did not chant her pagan song. Instead, she stood on the jutting rock, and threw the shadow of the cross upon the sown wheat.

When the seed did not germinate after the month was over, when she saw it was hopeless to wait for a miracle, Christina came down to the valley, and went to see Mort at the store.

She stayed a long time near the counter, not speaking. Once she started to say something, but someone came in, and she was silent again, long after the customer had gone.

It was Mort who broke the silence finally. He had gone to the rear of the store, in the deep shadows where stood the crates and the cartons of goods, and as he came back to the counter in front, he said,

"Christina, did the wheat come up?"

There was no irony in his voice. Only a pity that the big woman did not understand. Her face and hands were dirty, and her long yellow hair was matted by sweat. It fell stiffly against her shoulder, framing the square, ugly face. Her lips were pale. She shook her head. "No," she said, "it didn't come up."

"This is not wheat country," the storekeeper said gently. "You can grow some at the other end of the valley, where the river is. But not here, and much less up into the hills. I keep seed for people that grow wheat at the other end, but I never sold a bag to anyone around here."

She stood looking at him, her face stupid and tired. There were lines around her eyes. Her breathing had become audible in the silent store. She was like a great spent ox after the long pull home.

"That's the way it is, Christina," said Mort. "Me, I figure never to mind other people's business. But there you are. The wheat didn't come up. You couldn't ever grow wheat up there, Christina. You know that."

"Bill said. . . ."

But Mort stopped her with his raised hand.

"Sure! Bill dreamed. He dreamed often. I've listened to every one of his dreams. . . ."

"He was going to find some water, a spring in the mountains, channel it down to our place. . . ."

Mort shook his head and repeated, "He knew how to dream, Bill did. Why, he couldn't find water in the Barren Hills if he dug a thousand feet down. We hardly found any here, in the valley, thirty years ago."

He slowly rubbed the bald spot on his head and looked sadly at Christina.

"That's the way it is, Christina. No use trying. You're liable to kill yourself tilling that field up there, and nothing will ever come out of it. . . ."

She stood up again, facing him, a foot taller than he was.

The storekeeper blinked, pulled his glasses down on his nose, and looked at her over them.

"I been a friend of Big Bill a long time, Christina, you know that. Helped him all I could. What's your idea, why do you want to grow wheat? Place hardly big enough to grow a cash crop, and you can't feed your horse wheat in this country. . . ."

She leaned over the counter, her face close to Mort's.

"Don't you know why?" she asked. "Can't you see it? It's on account of how Bill dreamed. All about the wheat he'd grow, and then we'd get a place in the valley. I grew up near the green fields, and the golden fields of the ripe crops. I needed them. Bill knew that. He kept talking about the wheat we'd grow in our field. But he never got around to doing anything about it. He died, and now I've got to grow the wheat. . . ."

Mort nodded.

"You see," said Christina in her tense, hoarse voice, "you understand, don't you? Now I'll grow the wheat."

"You tried," said Mort, "and the wheat didn't come up. How you figure to do it now?"

He had no sarcasm in his voice, but again the deep pity for the woman who had to grow the wheat her husband had not known how to grow.

She had never spoken so much to anyone, and Mort felt a strange feeling of fear creep up his spine as he looked at her eyes, the grim face, the hard jaw.

"Can you understand hunger, Mort?" she asked. "This is a kind of it. Or wanting to win in a fight. No matter what the fight is about. Bill didn't grow the wheat, but I will. I tried your way, and the way of the people at the river end of the valley. I tried it. No one can say I didn't try hard. There'll be wheat on my field."

She was smiling now, but Mort did not like to look at the smile. Her eyes were not smiling.

Her hand fumbled in the bodice, and she took out a soiled paper, damp with the sweat of her breasts, and she smoothed it out on the counter, so Mort could read it.

He bent and studied the writing, but it was in a language he did not understand.

"What is it, Christina?" he asked.

She snatched the paper from the counter and put it back where she had taken it against her skin. She kept her hand there against the warm breast, as if seeking reassurance.

"Bill is dead," she said flatly, "he kicked me in the face, and he beat me when he was drunk, but I never lifted a finger to fight back. That was because I loved him. Now he's dead, and I'll grow the wheat he didn't get around to growing."

She bent down over the counter and her voice whispered to Mort, "This is the secret. The paper is the secret. It tells how to grow the wheat. You wouldn't know how, but now I do. It's a terrible secret. . . ."

Mort shrugged his shoulders.

"As you wish, Christina. I told you what I thought about growing anything up the mountain, or even down the valley. Maybe the secret doesn't work either. I figure that also is your business. . . ."

"But I had to tell you, Mort," she said. "I had to tell you about the secret. Now you know I tried the right way. No one can blame me for trying the other way. . . . Don't you see?"

She smiled again, the way Mort didn't like.

"Give me some seed wheat, Mort. I'll pay you later."

He stood undecided for a few seconds, then he shrugged his shoulders in the familiar gesture he had, and went to get the wheat.

When he came back from the hangar, dragging the bag along the floor, she lifted the heavy sack under her arm and silently walked out. He heard the horse riding away outside.

That night, Mort slept fitfully on the cot stretched behind the hardware counter. He kept thinking of the woman's smile, the paper in her bodice.

In the morning he saw that she was again at work in the small field, hoeing and sowing the new seed.

When darkness fell, the people of the town who had seen her come into Mort's store the day before, and ride away again, listened for her chanting to come down from the hills. But they did not hear it. All they heard was the gallop of the gelding—or was it some other horse?—through the village, long after they were in bed.

For Christina had sown the seed, and after she sat in the cabin waiting for the hour. When the hour came, she saddled the horse and rode it into town, along main street, as far as Luke's barber-shop, in front of Mort's store. She rode to the back of the building and crept inside through the unlocked back door.

She grabbed Luke before he could scream. The small, puny Irishman who had come from the East to open the barber-shop years ago could not fight the big woman's tremendous strength, and she gagged him securely before she trussed his hands and feet.

Then she carried him outside to the gelding.

Only one person saw her. Mort had heard the gelding ride into the village, and he had seen Christina leading the horse behind the barber-shop, for he had stayed at his window, watching the mountain uneasily, and the strange woman who tilled its soil. Later he saw her emerge from the back with her burden, and ride away into the night. And Mort, after that, could not sleep at all.

Christina frenzied the gelding with her stirrups, and the horse almost flew up the path to the lone cabin.

When she got there, she threw Luke on the ground, took a length of rope from her waist, and passed it under the shoulders of the man. He moaned under the gag, and writhed, but she paid no attention to him.

Then she tied the rope to the saddle of the gelding, and led the horse, dragging the man on the ground, to the field of new-sown wheat.

There she knelt beside Luke and ungagged him.

"You want to know why you're here?" she said. "It's you or

someone else. You're here because of the wheat. There's got to be wheat. I spent twenty years with Bill, waiting for him to grow wheat, but he didn't. Now he's dead. I can't go. I must stay with him here. So I'll grow the wheat. I may not grow a lot of wheat. Maybe only this crop. But it doesn't matter. It's a fight I got to win. A fight with the soil, and maybe with God. I have a paper here. . . ."

Luke saw the contorted face of the woman as she bent over him, and her eyes. He was shaking violently. When he tried to speak, it was only a ghoulish croak that came from his throat.

She didn't hear him. She was unfolding the paper she had taken from her bosom.

The moon pushed some clouds aside and came back to light the scene. The jagged rocks of the mountains stood out in the eerie light, and long shadows striped the flat valley.

"I don't need a light to read that paper," said Christina. "I know every word by heart. Long ago, in my country, I learned the secret that makes wheat grow. I listened to the songs of harvest time, and in winter I listened to the story-tellers night after night, sitting near the fire-place. And they all said the same thing, they told the tale of the Wheat God who knew how to make the grain grow anywhere, even on the rocky slopes, even where seed could never live. It's written on this paper, Luke. Listen, then you'll know why you're here."

She bent close to the small man on the ground.

"This year," she read, *"this year the wheat will grow and be beautiful because the earth has drunk the blood of man."*

And then she threw back her head and laughed a horrible laugh that hit the high rocks and echoed and moaned against the hills. Luke started screaming, a thin sound that rose in the night air when Christina's laugh had stopped travelling along the face of the mountain and into the valley below.

"My wheat will grow, Luke!" cried Christina.

She took a knife hanging from the horse's saddle, and bending down she cut the ropes binding the feet of the doomed man, carefully slitting the trouser leg. He tried to wriggle out of the shoulder ropes, every motion desperate, but the gelding moved, the rope went taut again, and he was powerless with his hands still bound.

Then Christina searched with her finger for the arteries on the legs, and in a sure stroke slashed them open.

Blood gushed out into the hoed earth. She ran to the horse, swung on it, and led the animal around the field, yelling her chant of triumph, reining the horse that the smell of blood made nervous. Dragged behind, Luke yelled with her, but it was in pure terror while his blood drained out, drenched the earth and the sown seed. Soon, his screams were fainter, and then they became a moan. Finally they stopped completely, as Christina turned the horse for the last time over the field.

Luke was quite still, horribly pale under the cold moonlight.

Mort heard the chant and the screams as he stood with the others in front of his store. They could not see the cabin in the darkness. They could only see the new fence reflecting the moonlight, up near the sky. But they couldn't see the cabin nor the field, only blurred shadows.

All evening Mort had watched. He was reluctant to clash with Christina, so when he saw her riding away with Luke, from his window, he didn't go out, didn't try to stop her. Instead he waited until she had gone up the path, then he went out to round up a few neighbours.

They were organizing the posse, debating on why Christina should kidnap Luke, when they heard the hoarse singing and the screams they recognized as those of the barber. They went up to the cabin, pushing the horses as fast as they could go on the dark, dangerous path. As they rode, Mort kept thinking of the paper with the strange markings Christina had shown him. He had not thought of Death, not in the plain unescapable words before, but now he did. He did as he recalled her words and her smile.

Half-way up, the screams became gradually fainter until they stopped.

They found Christina Sorensen sitting inside her cabin,

near the stove. She had lighted a small fire against the chill of the night, and she was rocking there, a wild look in her eyes, her mouth set in the grim smile.

"Where is he?" asked Mort as he walked into the cabin. "Where is Luke?"

Christina rocked contentedly and smiled at Mort.

"That was the way," she said. "The paper said how to do it. And I had been told of the strange way when I was a child. Now I'll get the wheat. That's all that matters."

The cabin was small, but of hewn logs. It was furnished with a table and two chairs, a dresser near a window, a wide cot in the corner.

There was a shelf next to the stove; the water pail stood there. The walls were bare. There was only a small picture of Bill tacked above the water shelf.

The men drew into a circle around the widow Sorensen. They had known what was in her eyes and now they were frightened.

She rocked in a steady rhythm, smiling at Mort.

He slapped her across the face, but she didn't move. She just wiped the blood that appeared on her lower lip.

One of the men walked out, and they could hear him going into the shed.

"He'll find him," said Christina suddenly. "You don't have to slap me any more, Mort."

They heard the yell, and when the man came in, he was dragging Luke's body. He let it drop at Christina's feet, the small, slight body of the bled man.

"He's dead?" asked Mort.

"Yeah," said the man flatly.

"Quite dead," said Christina.

She had not stopped rocking. Now she was smiling again.

"He bled to death!" said Mort.

They looked at each other, then at Christina.

"Blood," said the woman, stopping her rocking suddenly. "Blood. It was said on my paper that the wheat will be nice if the earth has drunk the blood of man. Look for nothing else. . . ."

The man who had found Luke ran out of the cabin, into the night, and he ran to the field below the cabin, and they heard his cries of disgust, and he ran back shouting curses, screaming at the mad woman.

"Goddam it, she bled him to death, all over the field! It's all wet with blood. It's Luke's blood!"

Christina spread her hands on her wide lap. Now she was rocking again.

"I told you to look for nothing else," she said.

They brought her down to Connor's Wells, and she didn't resist. She came silently, her head high, that strange smile still playing on her lips.

By morning, everyone knew of the horrible death at the widow's cabin, but the sheriff had posted guards at the jail door, and no one tried to take Christina away, although the feelings ran high in Connor's Wells.

For a week, the trial of the woman dragged. For a week, the widow sat in the box every time they called her in. She sat there and repeated the story of the earth that must drink the blood of man to feed the golden wheat.

She offered no defence and did not accept the lawyer the court offered her. Not once did she flare up in the terrible bursts of violence they expected of her.

Once she bowed her head and they could see tears running down her cheeks. It was when they mentioned Big Bill Sorensen, whom she had loved enough to stay there and *make* the wheat grow where it would not, instead of going to the places where wheat grew year after year and where she would have been happy.

The judge called a recess when he saw her cry, but when they reconvened, she was as calm as she had been before breaking down.

At the end of the week, the jury called her guilty of murder, and she was sentenced to hang in the courtyard two months later.

For two months, the people of Connor's Wells slept very badly. Every night, as dusk fell, they could see Christina, in her cell window, her arms stretched out in the form of a cross, looking at the field of sown wheat up against the mountain. And there she would chant her savage incantation, the words foreign to their ears. But they recognized the sounds that had kept them awake before, the sounds she had made high on the hill when Luke was bleeding to death.

One dawn of a clear morning, she was led to the scaffold they had erected during the night. All the people of Connor's Wells were there, lining the prison yard, standing on the wall, and those that couldn't come in were on the roofs of nearby houses. And the woman walked firmly up the thirteen steps, and she stood on the platform, facing the mountain beyond, the cabin that the rising sun showed clear and brown against the granite slopes, the small field. . . .

When the hangman held the hood over her head, and the sheriff asked her if she had anything to say before she paid for her crime, she pointed to the field and her great animal laughter shook the courtyard.

"Look!" she yelled, "Look up there, in my field! The wheat is growing!"

The hangman let the hood fall, and quickly secured the knot.

Then he kicked the trap open and the huge body fell, but they could hear the horrible laugh until the rope snapped her neck seven feet later.

And while she swung between the scaffold posts, the people turned and looked at the field up there above them, and they could see the wheat, the green stalks already strong in the morning breeze, a bright patch in the dreary yellow mountain as the sun played upon it, making it clearer than it had ever been, nearer. . . .

GRAHAM PETRIE

VILLAGE THEATRE

Bizarre events are most unsettling when they intrude into scenes of everyday life—as they do in the ingenious short stories of Graham Petrie. "I myself," he says, "see them as being on some borderline between the real and the unreal, often shifting back and forth within the same piece."

Petrie was born in Malaya and educated in England; he now teaches literature and film appreciation at McMaster University in Hamilton. He has written two books on film— The Cinema of François Truffaut *and* History Must Answer to Man: The Contemporary Hungarian Cinema *—as well as a widely praised, highly surreal novel,* Seahorse. *His stories have appeared in magazines ranging from* Playboy *to* Encounter.

THE village theatre is small and cramped: it is intended to seat an audience of perhaps a hundred, crowded together on ten rows of comfortless wooden benches, but during the performance of the play the spectators may number perhaps twice that, jammed as they are on one another's laps, squatting and sprawling in the aisles, crushed against the stage itself so that they can (and many of them do) reach out and take hold of a well-formed ankle or a shapely leg. The ushers having been instructed to admit everyone possessing tickets, the flourishing black market in forgeries that always establishes itself a good two months before the performance ensures that even the utmost compression of the audience into the limited space available will exclude several hundred indignant customers who parade outside, pathetically waving what they take to be authentic and valid permits. Matters have in fact reached such a pass that the village authorities are considering turning over to the forgers all responsibility for producing and selling tickets, and contenting themselves with claiming a small percentage of the profits realized—a sum that, in any case, far would exceed whatever they could hope to gain from the sale of a hundred or so legitimate admissions.

Among the audience for this particular performance are (let us call them) Dave and Elsie, a young couple from the city who have heard of the fame of the village play and, through a fortunate combination of circumstances, find themselves in possession of two genuine tickets as well as two seats within the theatre itself. They are sitting almost exactly in the centre of the crowd, in the sixth row from the front and squeezed together in the middle of the bench: the pressure of the bodies around them is so great that Elsie is almost perched on her husband's knee already and by the time the play begins she will definitely have been forced into that position. At the moment she is complaining bitterly about the excessive size of the head of the gentleman in front of her, though her future situation on Dave's lap will render this obstacle almost negligible, and will lead in turn to vociferous objections on the part of those unfortunate enough to be seated in the row behind her.

Elsie ignores these complaints: she is too busy squirming with excitement when at last (almost half an hour late) the curtain goes up to reveal the fabulous mechanism of the stage; and even Dave, mortified as he is to find that her wriggling body blocks off from his view all but a tiny fragment of the scene, cannot help but smile tolerantly at her enthusiasm. And now she can gaze her fill on the intricate combination of mirrors, set at all angles and corners of the auditorium, flashing multiple reflections of the audience at one another and on to the great central plate of glass that straddles the tiny stage and takes the place of the accustomed backcloth. She can glance upwards and to her right and see herself quite clearly; but the most fascinating thing of all is to see, beyond the expected limits of the stage, another audience, herself and Dave huddled in the very centre (or so she assumes, though she cannot yet distinguish them, the faces are so many) and, performing before that audience, moving with the same gestures, the same movements, the same rhythms, a duplicate set of actors!

The audience is quieter now, the preliminary buzz of wonder and excited comment has died away, and she and Dave can begin to make out some of the dialogue. She is quickly bored, however; the play is far above her head, some nonsense about a dramatist who writes a play predicting his own death and then, during a performance of that play, commits suicide on stage. So she ignores the words, the subtle and tortured motivations of the characters, and (like most of her fellow spectators) gives herself up to contemplation of the double panorama before her: the repetition of each facial expression, each gesture, introduces into the play a strange sense of formality, even of ritual, and the constant movement of each actor towards and then away from his mirrored counterpart imposes on the action the aspect of a courtly dance.

But even this too soon palls, so she turns her attention now to the imaged audience, trying in vain to isolate her own features and those of Dave from the mass of onlookers before her. They must be there somewhere, though, she is sure of that, for she can see, crowded round the stage, their backs turned to her, reaching out their hands to trip or impede the performers, a group of boisterous young men; and, staring back at them, their coarse, sly faces twisted into grimaces of complacent malice, are their spiritual and reversed twin brothers, with meddling left hand replacing right. At last she has to give up the search for herself, content to know that she is there; she adjusts herself more comfortably on her husband's knee and asks if he is satisfied. He nods, though in reality he has become as bored by the proceedings as she is: the play is totally incomprehensible and some of the more fortunate spectators at the very edge of the benches have already begun to slip away; from the corner of her eye, she can see them making a furtive exit from the theatre, accompanied, from beyond the back of the stage, by their faithful shadows.

Elsie envies them and wishes that they too had been lucky enough to secure such a fortunate position; their absence, however, has lessened the pressure along the benches and she finds that she has a seat to herself now and can allow Dave the relief of stretching his cramped and aching legs. And at the rate the benches are emptying around her, it will not be long before they too will be able to conduct a discreet withdrawal; she nudges Dave gently and nods towards the aisle, and is pleased to see him take the hint and begin to shuffle quietly towards the exit.

It is at just this point when a still courteous and relatively well-conducted retreat is about to degenerate into a boorish stampede that Elsie and her fellow spectators become aware of a significant alteration in the activity taking place on stage. This has, in fact, been going on for some time, but in an unobtrusive manner that has had little more effect than a momentary uneasiness in even the most observant watchers, a belated inquiry as to whether they were mistaken or not in seeing what they had appeared to see. Now, however, there is no more room for debate: in swift succession one, two, then half a dozen of the actors emerge from the area that, till this moment, all have assumed to be within the mirror, and begin to mingle with their fellows at the front of the stage. Then, with hardly a pause, they move in groups of two or three back across the dividing line that is thus confirmed to have been totally illusory all along! A gasp of surprise goes up from the audience; there is wonder in it, together with some natural rage and resentment at the trickery thus cunningly laid bare; and Elsie is forced to wonder whether the audience facing them, currently engaged in manifesting the same symptoms of delight and indignation, consists of innocent spectators in an auditorium the exact duplicate of her own, or a group of townspeople coached and rehearsed to carry through their parts.

The activity within the theatre has attracted the attention of those already crowding towards the exits; there follow several minutes of confusion as they struggle to turn back and regain the seats they have recently vacated, and even some of those beyond the doorway are drawn back inside the hall again by the commotion. As the renegades fight to reclaim their seats, Elsie finds herself jostled back along the bench to the position that she had previously occupied; she is content to accept this, however, and to attempt once more to extract some significance from the new configuration of forces upon the stage. No doubt anticipating a hiatus of this kind, the playwright has thoughtfully written a period of *temps mort* into his action: the characters shuffle around the stage exchanging conventional banalities until silence and order have been restored.

Now the deceptive movement of the play takes on another direction: scenery is introduced into the wings, leaving the centre of the stage bare and the two audiences still confronting one another. With a sudden thrill of excitement, Elsie recognizes the setting: it is the village itself, exactly as it appeared to her this morning, on her arrival! The couple emerging from the station could well be Dave and herself, though, on reflection, she recognizes that every other man and woman in the audience will make a similar identification. Then, almost imperceptibly, the scene changes to that of the theatre itself: somehow an almost exact replica has appeared, complete with audience and dangling mirrors, and, for a moment, Elsie finds herself searching for her counterpart on stage. Becoming aware of her naivety, she settles back on the bench and utters a low laugh; Dave, however, who has also been momentarily deceived, has become indignant: having studied Modern Drama, he is in a better position to appreciate the shallow and facile imagination that is at work here, the cheap and meretricious imitation of techniques that were once vibrant in the hands of others.

There is little more, however, for them to endure: having exhausted his repertoire of stale devices, the author seems determined to push quickly towards a conclusion: after a brief display of visual and verbal pyrotechnics, the lights dim on the playwright's corpse as it lies prostrate on the stage. When the lights go up once more and the actors step forward to take their bows (restoring the original mirror illusion, with one line facing the audience that contains Dave and Elsie and the other, with backs turned, receiving the plaudits of the false audience beyond the stage), Elsie notices that the dramatist's body has remained in its former position, exactly straddling the line that the central mirror would have occupied, had it existed, and that a stream of very realistic-looking blood is flowing from between his ribs. She tries to draw Dave's attention to her discovery, but her husband, angered by the ecstatic approval accorded by his fellows to this trivial and degrading spectacle, has seized her wrist and is dragging her towards the exit, shouldering aside those of the applauding spectators who happen to be in their way. Just before she is compelled to follow him through the doorway, Elsie takes a final, despairing glance at the stage and notices that in the extreme right-hand corner a young man is likewise dragging a young woman through the corresponding exit. She has little time, however, to ponder on the mania for detail that insists on prolonging the theatrical illusion far beyond its natural boundaries, for, as she steps through the doorway, she becomes aware that someone's hand has taken a firm clasp of her right ankle. Peering over the edge of the stage, and almost dazzled at first by the footlights, she recognizes the sly, coarse features leering up at her, and naturally enough, she begins to scream.

AL PURDY

THE UNDERTAKER

Al Purdy lives in Ameliasburg, a quiet little town near Belleville, Ontario, and has published more than a dozen collections of vigorous poetry—full of autobiographical particulars and evocations of the paleolithic past and the future of man among the stars. North of Summer, Being Alive, *and* The Stone Bird *are three such collections. It must have been rather disconcerting to his neighbours, then, when Purdy went around to his local undertaker and picked up all the fascinatingly macabre background for this horrific tale of the supernatural. But then, there comes a time for every man—as Purdy says in one of his poems—*

To travel deep in himself
To meet himself as a stranger
At the northern end of the world.

THEY were in love. Joe waited every week-day morning at the footbridge for Beth Holliday to meet him, and they walked the rest of the way to school together. In the warm summer evenings after homework was finished they strolled arm in arm beside the river, where an oily slick from the creosote works rainbowed the water. They had achieved the "going together" status, which conferred near-adult dignity among other teen-agers.

Beth was a very pale girl of Scandinavian origins. Her manner was serious, none of her schoolmates had ever seen her smile. Blue lakes for eyes, with blue shadows under them; blonde hair worn long—something of the remote princess, the Lady of Shalott. No mirror through which she saw the reflected world, but a heart condition served much the same purpose. Joe never did find out the medical language that characterized this mysterious frailness, and he did not ask. But it awed him, made him regard her with the solicitude of a naturalist for a rare and delicate species not far from extinction. He carried her school-books, elbowed a path through crowds at Saturday-night movies, continually interposed his chunky body and florid face between the tall pale girl and the muscular hurrying world.

Probably it was good for him. Joe was an unimaginative youth, but he felt something of a different fibre from himself in the girl; different also from the shrieking, giggling *ménage* of swaying teenage females at school football games. She talked of books, the poetry of John Keats and Shelley. The romance of Lancelot and Guinevere, Paris and Helen, Abelard and Heloise—people the bewildered Joe had never heard of. She accepted the red-faced homage he bestowed on her, not with any superiority but with a solemn eagerness all her own.

There was no doubt that in the pre-Joe years she had been

lonely. Medical restrictions prevented the usual games of childhood. Her own temperament as well as illness forced her into the introspection of books and music. And Joe was a red-faced wind devil who inexplicably stopped whirling in order to be near her. Once she asked him "Why do you like me?" Of course he hadn't been able to answer. "Because I don't laugh and run like the other girls?"

"I guess that's it," Joe said, searching his mind earnestly. "Why don't you laugh sometimes? That wouldn't hurt you, would it?"

"No, but I can enjoy things without laughing. My mother told me the things that make people laugh always come from doing something I can't do. They'd make my heart go too fast. So I got out of the habit of laughing." She looked at him anxiously. "Am I too serious?"

The great blue shadows of her eyes turned on him like deep lakes whose meaning was too transparent for Joe to fathom. She put her hand on his, the warm mysterious touch of her illness enthralling him. "If I kissed you," he blurted, "would it—would it —— ?"

"I don't think so. Do you want to?" Calmly she bent her white face down and touched his lips. Joe was astonished, for the sweet coolness of her face was like rain. It was not like being kissed by a girl at all, with hot freckles and snub nose mashed against his own sunburned face. He was so astonished he did not want to kiss her again, but went home more bewildered than ever by the mysterious attractions of Beth Holliday. His furious nature was stilled in her quietness. He bathed himself in her romantic fancies, cool dreams in which were infinite distances overhung by mists that never allowed him to see the ending of any story.

Gradually he came to feel he had arrived at the finish of a love-affair, but the end was the same as the middle and the beginning. As if they had been married a long time and grown old together, all their children gone away, leaving them the timeless calm of aftermath in which was no urgency, but a slow waiting for death. She was seventeen.

One day in school Joe noticed a pair of legs. They were brown, rather short legs, with a girl attached. She grinned at him and he grinned back. On the week-end they went swimming, Joe chasing her round and round the raft anchored a hundred yards from the beach. He chased her afterwards, down the narrow sandstrip in the sun, pursued her into moonlight, brown legs flashing ahead and waiting to be caught.

He left school that year, having developed sufficient speed of foot to overtake a succession of brown girls, freckled girls, red-lipped girls—pursuing them into streets and restaurants and sometimes grounding them at last in sunless, old-fashioned front parlours with "Thou shalt nots" prominent on faded wallpaper. But he did. For they were always caught. There was some cool quality about Joe's red face that attracted females. He didn't try to figure it out; all the nascent forces of adolescence bursting inside him at once allowed no time for such introspection.

The town's only undertaker at that time was old John Clegg, whose assistant had recently departed elsewhere to set up his own establishment. Old Clegg was touching seventy when Joe applied for a job, and not in the best of health either. Joe's junior matriculation certificate was the open sesame. He took up his new duties with zest and the peculiar coolness he had acquired before leaving high school. After two years of learning the rudiments and niceties of the embalming business at a school in Toronto (graduating second in his class), Joe took over more and more of the duties old Clegg had delegated to his previous assistant. He knew the exact mixture of glycerine and formaldehyde to pour into the round glass water-cooler and its pumping apparatus. He sterilized the knives and chrome instruments in the manner of one born to the job.

At first the cadavers had nauseated him. He had to retire to the bathroom when first witnessing the old man's deft slicing of a carotid artery, but recovered in time to assist at his own gruesome initiation. Old Clegg informed him that the carotid was the best place for insertion of a rubber tube that pumped embalming fluid into the corpse.

"Some says it ain't," the old man muttered, with liver-spotted hands steady on the dead man's neck. "But the carotid's a main artery, easy to find. Now watch!" Clegg slit the dead man's throat like a chicken's, cut into the red fruit-like arterial tissue, deftly inserting the rubber tube. "Now here's the jugular," he informed his apprentice with a grin. "It's right beside the carotid. Shove that other tube in there to take the blood as it gets pumped out by the embalming fluid coming in."

Joe's mouth and throat were dry, but he did as he was told. Clegg nodded approval. "Corpses don't mind much if you can't find that artery first time around, but it makes a messy job. Especially if it's a woman. Ya gotta make damn sure the incision is covered." He started the pumping apparatus, and Joe watched the level of pale, green embalming fluid descend in its round glass bowl. Later he poured the bucket of blood sloshing down the sink, rinsing afterwards.

Once in those early days of his apprenticeship there was a minor catastrophe. Joe forgot to place the tube carrying outgoing blood into a bucket provided for that purpose. Blood was filmed a quarter-inch thick on the floor when old Clegg noticed it, cursing Joe for his mistake with lucid amiability. After mopping and scrubbing for nearly an hour on that occasion, Joe was never so forgetful again.

Ten years after entering the undertaking business Joe was given his own nervous and shaking apprentice, and Clegg went into retirement. "You do all the work and I'll take the money," the old man cackled. "Sides, it's getting so my hands won't hold still long enough to do a job." He held the shaking liver-spotted hands up for Joe to inspect. "You'll be doin the same job on me one of these days." He looked at the younger man shrewdly. "You got any money? Enough to buy the business, I mean?"

Joe hadn't, but the bank was obliging enough to lend it to him at low interest rates. Two years later old Clegg died, and as the old man had predicted, Joe "did a job" on him. Standing in the imitation-mahogany-panelled chapel he considered business matters with some satisfaction. Appreciation of the young man's professional services was rising steadily. He attended the

United Church on Sundays (when not otherwise engaged), and sang a good strong tenor, which made the minister shake his hand approvingly after the sermon. Besides, Joe was able to throw a fair amount of business in the reverend's direction.

The church was an excellent place to make business and social contacts, Joe had found. In the coloured sunlight, shaped into curves and rectangles by the tinted glass windows, he sometimes allowed his eyes to rest on a charming face or trim legs, being careful to keep his chin poised at the same upward angle while doing so. Nothing like an undertaker for respectability, he reflected, his good tenor joining the gravel-throated congregation in "Throw out the Lifeline" — then settling down on the oak bench to mentally exclude the sermon, vacant eyes staring into space while the hard pinpoint of his mind centred on a girl's soft neck. She squirmed knowingly, and threw a glance over his shoulder in the midst of a rolling vowel, but Joe did not move a muscle.

Thinking of the girl in front of him, he suddenly remembered bringing in a fresh cadaver with old Clegg, stretching it out on the white enameled embalming table. He had touched the naked body, then jumped back startled. It was hot, almost like fire. The old man grinned. "Fresh beef, ain't had time to cool yet. Soon as anyone dies their temperature shoots up like a sky-rocket. Dunno why, but that's the way it is. Like they wanted to live some more an that was the oney way they could show it." Joe's eyes touched the short hairs on the nape of the girl ahead of him. She twitched in nervous awareness. Her neck looked flushed and hot.

After the service he spoke to the girl and her mother, shook their white gloved hands. Later he saw the mother whisper something to her daughter. He guessed what it was and grinned inside.

At the age of thirty Joe had become a well-rounded figure in his grey trousers and dark jacket. His face was still a healthy red, with blunt features, a manner at once cordial and slightly withdrawn as became his profession. Perhaps the old schoolboy romance with Beth Holliday had something to do with him remaining single. Sometimes he saw her go by the chapel on her way to work at the library. She was in charge of children's books, presiding over fairy-tales and science for young people with blonde serenity. She always went by the chapel going to and from work, passing on the opposite side of the street and carrying an umbrella whether it was raining or not. He wondered about it once, that umbrella. Perhaps for protection against male advances. He smiled to himself. All that hogwash about Lancelot and Guinevere. The stainless knight of the round table she had expected him to be. The mystery of an illness that was without outward symptoms, but left her invalid within. That was probably hogwash too. She was no use to any man.

Every afternoon she walked by the chapel at ten minutes after five, passing under the big chestnut tree with pale serious face, a little thinner now, hands clutching an umbrella. He thought of his latest girl-friend, comparing the two of them feature by feature. But there was really no comparison at all. Sylvia was dark, all fire and thumping passion, with big white pillows of breasts for a man to lie between. Sometimes she'd bite while they were making love, and bite hard. Later he'd ask her to keep her teeth away from his carotid artery, explaining its significance in his profession. They'd both laugh. It had been a stock joke with Joe for years now.

Lately he'd taken to using the little room off the chapel for his assignments. The room was actually meant for mourners who found themselves a little overcome while paying their last respects to a dear one, but the couch was very useful for erotic passages as well. And he'd discovered the atmosphere of the chapel to have a stimulating effect which caused his partners to give of their best. Naturally such extracurricular guests had to enter by a rear door, left unlocked by pre-arrangement.

Joe sighed a little. Perhaps he was tired of Sylvia's full-blown charms. There'd been a new girl in town for the last few days, a waitress at Joe's Café. Came from Montreal, she said, though he didn't believe it. She sounded too much American, a teasing trace of the deep south in her voice, like a cream-fed cat.

Her name was Julie. He thought she might be in the country illegally at first, but scoffed at himself for the idea. What American girl would enter Canada illegally? Still, working in a joint like Joe's Café! For Joe Barona was a real tough nut. He'd tried to get him to change the name of the restaurant a while back. It might remind people of the Eternal Rest Chapel and its new proprietor. But Joe Barona wouldn't change a thing. He thought of the black-jowled Italian with distaste.

Julie, working at Barona's dingy little greasy-spoon — slender Julie with bold eyes and broad hips, dishing up chow for small-town customers. People looked at Julie and sometimes forgot all about their food. A dish. The kind you don't meet in church. He frowned. She'd said no to him twice. But that was to be expected. No girl wants to look easy, and Joe never minced words after a certain stage in his ritual courtship. He put it right on the line. Not baldly stated in so many words, but nevertheless unmistakable. A combination of oblique words and bold admiring glances — Julie would succumb eventually, he was sure.

Outside the sky was black, thunder smacking its lips high among the clouds. Rain began to fall in great drops. A long bar of sunlight touched the green chestnut leaves across the street. It reminded Joe, standing just inside the chapel door, of the stained green glass light in church. But here there was no girl, no sensitive white neck for the sunlight to touch and make aware of his glance. The thought was still unfinished when he saw Beth Holliday coming from the end of the block. Before she reached the chestnut tree black skies unbolted and rain came down in solid sheets. The girl came to a sudden halt under the tree, rain pouring outside the chestnut's periphery, weird green light piercing the leaves and resting on her blonde head. She was pretty wet, Joe noted with a twinge of pity. She'd forgotten her umbrella too. He half-turned to go back in the shop and find her an umbrella, then stopped. It might mean the beginning of something for which he had no taste any longer. He stood hidden behind the curtain watching her, while the rain poured.

Beth looked towards the chapel once, pale and serious, the

blue shadows under her eyes enlarged enormously. He could see her clearly from the chapel, as if they had been walking across the footbridge together in an earlier rainfall, pearl beads of water spangling her hair, Joe carrying her books as before. Lancelot and Guinevere. Again he turned to get her an umbrella, and came back just in time to see the girl running away down the street. It was the first time he had ever seen her running, the very first time.

Next day was Tuesday, fair and bright, the sky washed clear of rain. Joe and his assistant received a call from the small local hospital in the morning. He was to pick up the body of Beth Holliday. An intern explained what had happened as they wheeled the stretcher into position. "Rheumatic heart," he said tersely. "She got caught in the rainstorm yesterday, and ran to get home. Her heart wouldn't take that sort of thing." The intern slapped his hands together expressively and said, "Whoof!"

Once, before they reached the embalming room, he touched her hand. It was fiery hot. He recoiled as if from a leper, noticing his assistant eye him curiously. "Body heat goes up immediately after death," Joe explained, and found himself echoing old Clegg almost word for word. "Don't know why—it's like she wanted to live some more, and that was the only way to show it." He blinked, not tears, for he didn't feel grief exactly. Just blinked rapidly, and thought of yesterday, her standing in the rain, himself inside. If he'd got that umbrella for her right away, without waiting to think about it, she might be alive—— He shrugged himself out of the mood quickly. Just the same it was hard to believe she was dead, even with the draped evidence of her body in front of him.

Later he gave his helper the rest of the day off, seeing the young man's eyes turn knowledgeable and wise. But that couldn't be helped. He prepared the embalming fluid slowly, shaking his head with dogged wonder at himself. Things he hadn't thought of for years—the girl holding onto his arm, exclaiming at some trifling colour of leaf she'd seen, wanting him to notice it also. The trust she'd had in him, something he hadn't realized at the time, but remembered now. Not really a human girl, for she'd asked nothing from life, and that was exactly what she'd got. But how could he know that without looking into her mind, a thing he'd never done?

Naked on the white table Beth Holliday lost no dignity, as if long-expected death had not changed her in any essential way. Awkwardness suggested by clothing was erased, her limbs were liquid white, and belonged to her body like the joined arms of the same moonlit sea. Joe muttered something, listened in on himself to find out what he was thinking. "She can't be dead," he heard—but she was. Closed eyes with night-blue shadows, serious sweet mouth, pale gold nipples pointing up at the glaring eye-like two-hundred-watt bulb, pale pale pubic hair mounded impregnably for ever now. He could have wept for himself, but a moment later he had lost the capacity again.

Joe was sometimes a furious man, and anger seized him. He took his steel instruments and slit the white throat, finding the carotid with practised certainty, listened to the low chugging of the electric pump pushing her blood into a galvanized bucket. It made a quiet slurping sound, like a large amount of tomato soup in the mouth of a fat man.

He went out afterwards and drank a bottle of rye whisky. Then went round to his namesake's café to see Julie. The slender perhaps American girl made half-promises, but no firm commitment. Joe was surly. "Okay," he told her. "I been drinkin'. Sometimes I do drink a little too much. But it makes no difference. You know I want you——" And she did know. But Joe didn't look so respectable at this moment. His face was a bright crimson shade from the whisky, though strangely this seemed to make his blunt features almost handsome with the virility of blood and fascination of that neutrality pact undertakers have with death. He explained to her about the unlocked door of the chapel building. She smiled, her objections seeming to give way suddenly. "All right, I'll come."

"You won't be scared?" he asked. The girl said no, she was not afraid. And he knew from her eyes that she was not. "After midnight then. I'll be waiting." With no more words he left.

All next day the few friends and acquaintances of Beth Holliday filed into the funeral chapel, signed their names in the book, and went solemnly away. Some of them gave Joe a remembering look, but he ignored the glances, stiffly erect in grey trousers and neat dark jacket, so drunk he could scarcely stand. At eleven o'clock that night he locked the front door and went to get another bottle of whisky before Julie arrived. He managed to obtain only a small twelve-ounce bottle from the town bootlegger, drank half of it in an alley, and shoved the bottle in his pocket. His mind kept going back to the pale dead girl in her wooden box, surrounded by flowers. "Guinevere," he snarled aloud. "Guinevere, and her damned umbrella." He drank the rest of the mickey in one gulp, heaving the bottle down the middle of the dark empty street. No heads popped out of windows to investigate the clattering sound. The town was asleep, only a vague light here and there behind misty curtains.

Joe went down the alley behind the undertaking parlour, entering the rear door. He flung off his coat, then stumbled over a chair on his way to the mourners' room. "Too early," he said drunkenly to himself. "She won't be here yet." But she was. A naked girl rose to meet him in the darkness, the street-light outside projecting tiger stripes through the steel blinds, marking the girl's flesh as if she were a beast. As perhaps she was. For he felt her claws and teeth. The gyrating hips that plunged at him, grating on pelvic bones, made this touching of bodies as much combat as love passage. "Julie," he muttered, "you're a bitch." He seized her arms and bore her down on the couch.

Drowned in sticky sweat and the musky smell of coupling, he could not think of the dead girl any longer. Julie held him tightly, the swift unison of their plunging movement pushing them together and apart like the courtship of sweating ghosts. There was a brief resistance at first, but over quickly—The pleasure of having his mind blanked out, physical sensation replacing thought, an epileptic freedom that battered at walls of darkness. The girl's body anticipated every movement of his own, a slight hesitation before the downstroke, herself surging up to meet him and hovering momentarily, as if it were a mating of birds in mid-air. Orgasm—all his teeth magically transferred to the loins, and a mediaeval dentist was pulling them out rapidly, violently, one by one—the bones of his body dissolved in a last convulsive spasm, leaving his flesh collapsed like a limp umbrella spread over the girl.

He felt a fainting sickness suddenly come over him, and broke away from her. "I'll be right back, honey," he gasped, running to the bathroom in the rear to pour cold water over his head. When he returned a few seconds later she was gone. Without questioning the girl's disappearance he dropped exhausted onto the couch and slept.

Next morning the sun came up. Joe struggled groggily from the couch, feeling beaten all through his body, but strangely light-headed. He lifted the steel blinds to examine the couch carefully, but the red velours showed nothing. When the young assistant came to work Joe told him to look after things and went back to sleep. At nine o'clock the phone rang, someone for Joe. He got into his clothes hurriedly, dashing into the office under the staring eyes of his helper.

It was Julie. "Joe," she said, "Joe?"

"Ya, whadda ya want?"

"I'm sorry, Joe."

"You're sorry?"

"I said I'm sorry. I just couldn't make it last night."

"What!"

"I couldn't make it. Listen, I'll come tonight Joe. I'll be there for sure tonight. You're not mad, Joe? Joe—"

He left the phone lying on the desk gargling to itself, and went back to the chapel where the pale girl was lying in her wooden box, surrounded by a kingdom of flowers. He saw that she was smiling.

BRIAN MOORE

THE SIGHT

Brian Moore has many allegiances—to Ireland, his country of birth; to Canada, his adopted country; and to the United States, where he now lives. Yet his greatest allegiance is to his own vision of the spirit of man. "If my work shows a bleak vision, it is simply Irish in that. The Celt always sees the worm and the spectre when he looks at the head of a man and it is that sense of hopelessness, and the feeling that man's life is ultimately useless, that has produced the literature." In addition to psychological novels like The Lonely Passion of Judith Hearne *and* The Luck of Ginger Coffey, *he has written a science-fiction novel* (Catholics), *a work of fantasy* (The Great Victorian Collection), *and a novel of terror* (The Mangan Inheritance). *The story here, which walks the fine line between the normal and the paranormal, is a chilling vision of "the worm and the spectre" in the mind of man.*

BENEDICT Chipman never took a drink before five and never drank after midnight. He ate only a light lunch, avoided bread and potatoes, and drank decaffeinated coffee. These self-regulations were, he sometimes thought, the only set rules he observed. Otherwise, he did as he liked.

Yet on the morning he returned to his eight-room apartment on Fifth Avenue after four days in hospital, his first act was to tell his housekeeper to bring some Scotch and ice into the library. When she brought it, he was standing by the window, looking out at Central Park. He did not turn around.

"Will that be all, sir?"

"Yes, thanks, Mrs. Leahy."

Chipman was fifty-two and a partner in a New York law firm. A few weeks ago, during his annual medical check-up, his doctor had noticed a large mole on his back and had recommended its removal. The operation was minor but, for Chipman who had never been in hospital before, the invasion of his bodily privacy by doctors, nurses, and attendants had been humiliating and vaguely upsetting. Then, to complicate matters, while the biopsy showed the mole to be probably benign, the pathologist advised that "to be completely sure", the surgeon should repeat the procedure but, this time, make a wider incision. The second biopsy had been scheduled for the end of the month. "There's nothing to worry about," the surgeon said. "Just relax and come back ten days from now."

But Chipman did not feel like relaxing. He felt nervous and irritable. As he poured the Scotch, he looked at the tray containing his mail. The first letter on the pile was postmarked Bishopsgate, N.H. He had been born in Bishopsgate and for some reason he could not explain the sight of the postmark disturbed him. The letter was from his brother, Blake, who wrote that he and his wife were coming to New York to visit their son Buddy, a journalism major at Columbia. Buddy, it seemed, had learned that his uncle had been in hospital and Blake wrote that all three of them would like to call tomorrow afternoon. The letter irritated Chipman. He had no wish to see Blake and his family. He thought of his brother as a man who had never in his life owned a hundred dollars he didn't know about and whose relations with himself were sycophantic rather than fraternal, largely because of loans which Blake had not repaid.

At the library door, Mrs. Leahy announced herself with a small prefatory cough. "Mrs. Kirwen is here, sir."

"Show her in. And ask if she'd like something to drink."

As he put his brother's letter down and rose to greet Geraldine, he heard her chatting with Mrs. Leahy in the front hall.

"Is *he* having one? Oh, well then, a sherry, I think. By the way, how's your nephew, Mrs. Leahy?"

"He still has the pleurisy, ma'am. But he'll be all right."

"Good, that's good news."

"Thank you, Mrs. Kirwen."

I never knew Mrs. Leahy had a nephew, Chipman said to himself. But, come to think of it, he didn't know much about Mrs. Leahy, although she had been with him for almost ten years. Lately, he had decided that his interest in other people was limited to the extent of their contributions to his purse, his pleasure, or his self-esteem. He had a weakness for such aphoristic judgements. But in this instance he also remembered another aphorist's warning: lack of interest in others is a first sign of age.

"Ben, darling, how are you? Shouldn't you have your feet up or something? You mustn't overdo it on your first day home."

"Stop fussing."

"I'm not fussing. Dr. Wilking told me you should take it easy."

"When was Wilking talking to *you*?"

"I met him in the corridor yesterday. Remember, he thinks I'm your wife."

The surgeon, who did not know Chipman, had come in on them unexpectedly the night after the biopsy and found Geraldine, the buttons of her dress undone, lying on the hospital bed with Chipman. The surgeon had tactfully assumed she was Chipman's wife and had addressed her as such in the subsequent conversation. No one had contradicted him. "That was a mistake," Chipman said now, remembering. "I should have said something."

"Oh, what's it matter?"

"Well, my own doctor, Dr. Loeb, knows I'm not married."

"Oh, Ben. Who cares nowadays?"

At that point Mrs. Leahy brought Geraldine's sherry. Geraldine, sipping it, put her long legs up on a yellow silk footstool. In this posture her skirt fell back, revealing her elegant thighs. Although impromptu erotic views normally pleased Chipman, this morning he was not pleased: he was irritated. "Why can't you sit properly?"

"That's not a very nice thing to say when I've given up an important job to be with you today."

"What job?"

"Remember I tried out for the Phil Lewis show last week? Well, my agent called and said they want me for a second audition this afternoon. He says that usually means you've got the job. But, I'm not going."

"Why not?"

"Because if I got the job it would mean I'd be on the coast for the next seven weeks. I'm not going to be three thousand miles away while you're in and out of hospital."

"I'm not in and out of hospital. I'm just going back for a couple of days, that's all. Now, be a good girl. Phone and say you'll be glad to audition this afternoon."

"No," she said, suddenly looking as though she might begin to cry.

"But why not?"

"Because I've realized something, Ben. I'm in love with you. I don't want to be separated from you."

In love with him? He remembered La Rochefoucauld's maxim that nothing is more natural or more mistaken than to suppose that we are loved. He knew Geraldine did not love him. She was an unsuccessful young actress, divorced from a television producer and in receipt of a reasonable alimony. His own role in her life was that of a suitable escort, an older man capable of providing presents and a good time, a friend who was good for a small loan and might not expect to see his money again. This sudden protestation of love was, he decided, no more than the familiar feminine need to justify having gone to bed with him. Geraldine would not give up her alimony: he did not want her to. The present arrangement suited him perfectly.

Nevertheless when she said that she loved him, for one moment he felt strangely elated. Then put his glass back on the silver tray and in its surface saw his face, which seemed distorted, white, old. This foolishness must stop. "Now, don't talk nonsense. Go and phone those people."

"Are you trying to get rid of me?"

"Of course not. But if you go out to Hollywood this week it might work out very well. I was thinking of going to Puerto Rico. I thought I'd take a vacation. Lie in the sun until I have to go back into hospital."

"Do you know people in Puerto Rico, is that it?"

"No. No. Look, Geraldine, you're *not* in love with me. My God, I'm twenty years older than you."

"Age has nothing to do with being in love with someone."

"Maybe not at your age. But at my age it has everything to do with it. Now go and make that phone call. Then I'll take you out and buy you lunch."

She stood and picked up the otter coat he had helped pay for, trailing it behind her on the carpet as she moved across the room. At the door, she turned. "So that's what you want? To go to Puerto Rico alone?"

"Yes."

"Okay."

She went into the hall. He listened to hear the tinkle as she picked up the phone, but instead heard the front door slam. He started across the room, thinking to go after her and bring her back, but stopped. He realized that he was close to the almost forgotten sensation of tears. Dammit, he'd just invented Puerto Rico to help her make up her mind about the audition. But now, as he felt himself tremble with anger—or was it weakness?—he decided a short vacation in the sun might be the ideal way to wait out the next ten days. Maybe with Geraldine. He decided to suggest it at the office when he went in tomorrow.

There might be a little ill-feeling, though. He had already had a long vacation this summer. But what could they do? In the seventeen years he had been a member of the firm he had frequently demonstrated that his interests were not the law or the success of the partnership, but women, music, and his collection of paintings. However, on the day he joined the partnership he brought with him, as a wedding present from his father-in-law, an insurance company which dwarfed all other clients the firm did business with. And although his marriage had subsequently broken up (his wife died eight years later in an alcoholic clinic, driven there, some said, by Chipman's behaviour with other women) his father-in-law had not held it against him. He still represented the insurance company and this power, coupled with his disregard for the firm's other clients, had driven his partners to revenge themselves on him in the only way they knew. They no longer invited him to their homes or, indeed, to any social function. Their boycott amused him: they bored him. They knew that he was amused and bored. Their dislike of him, he guessed, had long ago turned to hatred.

Yet on the following morning when he went to the office he was surprised to see George Geddes, the senior partner, come in at his doorway, eager, out of breath, and smiling like a job applicant. "Ben, how are you, how're you feeling?"

"Hello, George."

"So, how did it go?"

Directly behind Geddes, Chipman's secretary was at her

desk in the outer office. He did not want her to hear what he had to say and so beckoned Geddes in and shut the door. "Matter of fact, George, I wanted to have a word with you about that. Everything went very well, but they want me to go back, just as a precaution, and have a wider excision made. They've scheduled it for the thirty-first. I don't know. I'm feeling a little knocked out. I thought, if you don't mind, I might go and lie in the sun for a week. Not really come back to the office until next month."

As he spoke he noticed that Geddes was already nodding agreement as though helping someone with a speech impediment. "Of course, Ben, of course. No sense sitting around here. Good idea."

"Well, thanks. Of course there are a few things I can clear up before I go."

"No, no," Geddes said. "Let the juniors do some work for a change. Get on your feet again, that's the main thing."

After Geddes had left, Chipman phoned a travel agency. He booked a double room with patio and pool in a first-class Puerto Rico resort hotel, starting the following Monday. He called in his juniors and reviewed their current handling of his clients' affairs. At noon he told his secretary that he was leaving and would not be back until the first week in December. Then he took a taxi to his apartment and for the second morning in a row broke his rule and made himself a drink.

But now his reason was celebratory. What a relief it had been to find Geddes agreeable for once. And there was a note saying Geraldine had telephoned. Obviously, her temper tantrum had not lasted. After pouring a Scotch he picked up the phone and dialled her number.

"Geraldine? Ben. First of all, I'm sorry about yesterday."

"No, darling, it was my fault. Why shouldn't you go on a trip if you want to? When are you going, by the way?"

"No, tell me first, how was your audition?"

"I didn't go. It's a long story, I won't bore you with it."

"Does that mean you might be free to join me in Puerto Rico?"

"Ben, do you mean it?"

"Of course. I booked a double room with patio and pool in the Caribe Imperial. Or would you rather I got you a room of your own?"

"No, no."

"Good. And what about the week-end? Are you free?"

"Do you mean now? Yes. Completely."

"Well, so am I. Or, almost. I have to be here tomorrow afternoon when my brother and his family are coming. But that shouldn't take more than an hour."

"Are we thinking of the same thing?"

"I hope so."

"All right, darling. Come on down. I'll be waiting."

"I'll be right there."

His brother's hand, tentative at first, went out to finger the Steinway's polished surface, then boldly stroked the wood. His brother's head turned, afternoon sunlight merciless on the thin grey hair, the pink skull-cap of skin beneath. His brother smiled, ingratiate and falsely intimate. "Beautiful piano, eh, Ben?" his brother said. "You must play something for us before we go. I mean, if you feel up to it."

"Oh yes, Ben, you must," said his brother's wife who, he knew, did not care at all for music.

If he felt up to it. What would they say if they knew he had come up from the village two hours ago after a night of screwing that would exhaust anyone? Perhaps it would not exhaust Blake's wife, though. One summer, when their son Buddy was still a brat in rompers, Chipman had gone to visit them at their summer cottage on Cape Cod. He was sunbathing in the dunes when Blake's wife came up from the beach, drying her hair on a towel, her shoulder-straps undone, her swimsuit wet from the sea. She did not see him until she stumbled on him and when he reached up and pulled her down she did not say a word. Later they walked hand in hand over the dunes towards the cottage. Blake was sitting on a deck-chair on the lawn, reading a book, and the child was on the porch playing with an old inner tube.

Man and child looked up and his brother's wife at once let go of his hand and ran to kiss her child. She avoided Chipman for the rest of that evening and the following morning he thought it wise to pretend a business engagement in Boston. He had not been to stay with them since.

"Let Buddy play something," he said, knowing that Buddy's atrocious playing would please them much more than his own. And so Buddy obediently flopped down on the piano bench, looked disdainfully at the music scores in front of him, then poised his large hands over the keys. "What'll it be, Uncle Ben?"

"You choose," Chipman said. Years ago, prodded by Blake's wistful hints about the child's musical inclinations, he had paid for a series of piano lessons for Buddy. The money had been wasted for Buddy's musical talents were a myth, the first of a long series of efforts on his parents' part to make Chipman feel a special affection for the boy. All had failed. Buddy's only effect on his uncle was to relieve him of any regrets about not having had a son of his own.

But now he pretended to listen as Buddy stumbled through some Cole Porter tunes, noticing as he mimed attention that Buddy's parents seemed nervous as though they had quarrelled before coming and were now trying to cover it up by a surfeit of polite remarks to each other. Chipman was uninterested. He simply wanted them to go and so, when Blake glanced at last in his direction, he pretended drowsiness. It worked. As his son thumped to a pause in the music, Blake stood up. "Thanks, Bud, but we'd better not overtire your uncle. Besides, your mother and I want to catch that Wyeth show at the Met before our train leaves."

Then he turned to Chipman. "Ben, could I have a word with you?"

As on signal both Buddy and his mother left the room. It was, Chipman knew, the usual prelude to Blake's asking for money, but today a loan seemed well worth it to get rid of them. He went to his desk, aware that Blake, if left to his own devices, would take at least five minutes to come to the point. He opened a drawer and took out his cheque-book.

"What's that for?" Blake asked sharply.

"Nothing."

"Put that away, will you," Blake said. "I'm ashamed that I owe you so much. As a matter of fact, Ben, it wasn't that at all. It was just that we wondered if you'd like to come up to Bishopsgate to convalesce until you go back into the hospital."

"Thanks, but I'm going to Puerto Rico."

"Oh. Puerto Rico?"

"Yes, I thought I'd like to lie in the sun for a few days."

"Oh, that's a pity, we were looking forward to the thought of having you. You and I haven't spent much time together these last years."

"I know. Well, maybe some other time."

"Any time," Blake said. "I'd like us to go for walks around the old place and have talks and all that. I'd like that a lot."

And then, abruptly, Blake took hold of his hand and squeezed it. "I'd really like it, Ben."

"Well, we'll do it," Chipman said, uneasily, beginning to move towards the hallway where the others waited. As they came out he saw Blake's wife glance at her husband and saw Blake give a small, almost imperceptible shake of his head. Buddy came forward, hand out, smiling. "Good-bye, sir."

"Good-bye," Chipman said. "Good-bye, Blake."

His sister-in-law came towards him. He held out his hand. She ignored it and reached up to kiss him on the cheek. He was astonished. "Good-bye," his sister-in-law said. "Take care of yourself."

The elevator came. They went down.

Confused, Chipman closed the door of his apartment. It was as though he had found an interesting passage in a dull book and had seen it snatched away before he had time to finish it. Why had Blake's wife kissed him, she who had so carefully avoided kissing him ever since that summer on the beach? And why had Blake come up with this unprecedented invitation to visit them at Bishopsgate? Why were they being so kind all of a sudden? Come to think of it, everyone had been abnormally kind these past two days—Geraldine, Geddes, Blake. It was irritating, dammit, to be treated as though, all of a sudden, he were made of glass. How did La Rochefoucauld put it? *Pride does not wish to owe, nor vanity to pay.* He didn't want favours from anyone. So, why did they try?

He had reached the library door before the thought and the answer came to him. He was going to die. That was why they were all being so gentle. They knew something he didn't know. A wider excision, that was what the surgeon said. "To be completely sure," the pathologist said. They hadn't told him the truth, that was it. "Just relax," the surgeon said.

He must not panic. He must call Dr. Loeb, his internist, and put the question to him quite casually, implying that he already knew all about it. He must go to the phone now and clear things up.

He went into his bedroom and closed the door so that Mrs. Leahy would not overhear him. He phoned Dr. Loeb but the answering service said Dr. Loeb was out of town for the weekend and a Dr. Slattery was taking his calls. So that was no use. The surgeon's name was Wilking. He looked up the number. The answering service said Dr. Wilking wasn't in, but would he leave a message. He left his name and number and lay down on the bed, worrying. After five minutes he telephoned again and said it was an emergency. He must reach Dr. Wilking at once. This time, the answering service gave him a number to call. Dr. Wilking answered.

"Dr. Wilking, this is Benedict Chipman speaking. Now, I know this may sound silly to you, but was there anything about that operation of mine that I should know about?"

"Why do you ask, Mr. Chipman?"

"I just want to know the truth. It's important, doctor."

"Well, look, Mr. Chipman, it's pretty much as I told you. I don't think you have anything to worry about."

"Is that the truth? I want the truth."

"Yes, what can I say? Look, Mr. Chipman. The best thing you can do now is relax. Your wife mentioned you might go off for a short vacation. I think that's a good idea."

"How the hell can I take it easy? For God's sake, doctor, that's like telling a man to take it easy in the condemned cell while you decide whether or not he's to be reprieved."

"Oh, come on now, Mr. Chipman, I wouldn't say that."

"Of course, you wouldn't," Chipman shouted. "And that girl isn't my wife, do you hear? So anything you have to say, just say it to me!"

He put the receiver down without waiting to hear the surgeon's reply. He looked at his bed. This was the bed he might die in. He turned from it and went into his library. Small picture-lights lit his collection of Krieghoff landscapes. When he died these pictures would be sent to the Bishopsgate Art Gallery to be exhibited in a special room with a brass plaque over the door, identifying him as their donor. They would arrive after his body, which would be buried under a plain headstone in the episcopal cemetery, next to his parents' grave. How many people ever read donor's plaques or the names on headstones? A year from now he would be forgotten.

But wasn't that jumping the gun, giving in to a bad case of jitters unsupported by any evidence? How could they know he was going to die when they hadn't even done the second biopsy yet? What were they keeping from him? Whatever it was had frightened Geraldine into suddenly declaring her love. But she doesn't love me, Chipman decided, she pities me. Pity is what everyone feels for me now: Geraldine, Geddes, Blake, Blake's wife. Yet how could they all know this thing about me? Geraldine has never met Geddes. Or Buddy. Who told Buddy, for instance?

Chipman went to his desk, searched it, and then went to the telephone table in the hall. He knew he had a number for Buddy someplace, and when he found it and dialled it, it was a fraternity house. No one answered for a long time and then some boy told him Buddy wasn't in, and that he didn't know when he would be back. As Chipman replaced the receiver, Mrs. Leahy passed him in the hall, going down the corridor to her own room. Only one person might have spoken to Buddy, to Geddes, to Geraldine. One person who would answer the phone when people called here to ask how he was. He went down the corridor to the far end of the apartment and stopped outside Mrs. Leahy's door. He almost never came into this part of the apartment, near the pantry and wine cellar, and past the kitchen. He stood for a moment and then, without knocking, he opened the door.

He had not seen the inside of Mrs. Leahy's room for years. Sometimes he heard the television sound, turned low, and sometimes she would leave the door open, at night, when she went to answer the phone. Now, his eyes went from the television set to the horrid rose and green curtains, the cheap coloured lithograph of some saint, to the crucifix, entwined with fading palm, which hung over what seemed to be a sewing-table. It was the sort of room he used to glimpse through upper-storey windows, years ago, when he still rode the subways, a room which screamed a sudden mockery of all other rooms in his elegant apartment. And its occupant, her back to him, unaware of his presence, was the perfect figure in this interior. In her pudgy fingers, the surprise of a cigarette: on her lap, inevitably, the garish headlines of the *Daily News*.

"Mrs. Leahy?"

She turned. Her grey head was that of a stranger's, utterly changed by the absence of her uniform cap. "Oh, did you ring, sir? Is the bell not working?"

"No, I didn't ring."

"Can I get you something, sir? Are you all right?"

By this time she had stubbed her cigarette and had pinned on the familiar housemaid's cap. "A little whisky?" she said. "Or, are you hungry, sir? Would you like a sandwich?"

"Whisky," he said. "And I want to talk to you."

"Yes, Mr. Chipman." Swiftly she moved past him going down the corridor to the monastic neatness of her kitchen. She did not, of course, expect him to follow her into the kitchen and looked up, surprised, when he did.

"A little water with it, sir? I'll bring it into the library, will I?"

"No. Sit down, Mrs. Leahy. Please."

As she placed the bottle of Scotch, ice, and a glass and pitcher of water on a tray, he drew out one of the chrome and leather kitchen chairs, indicating that she should sit in at the table. As she did, he saw a red rash of embarrassment rise from her neck to her cheeks. They had never been informal together. He sat opposite her and poured himself a Scotch. "Now," he said. "Let me ask you something. Are you the person who's been telling people I have cancer?"

"Me, sir?"

"Yes, you."

She did not answer him at once. She put her veiny old hands on the table, joined them as in an attitude of prayer, then looked at him with the calculating, ready-to-bolt caution of a rodent. He had never before noticed this animal quality of hers. Why, she's a hedgehog, he decided. She's Mrs. Tiggy-winkle.

"Yes, sir. It was me."

He must keep calm. He must not let her know that he was ignorant of all the facts of his illness. "I see. And who told *you* that I might have cancer?"

"Mrs. Kirwen, sir."

"And what did she say, exactly?"

"Ah, she didn't say you had cancer, she said they were going to operate on you again just to be sure. There was always the chance, she said. And I said to her I thought I should let Mr. Buddy know. On account of your brother, sir. And then Mr. Geddes rang up about you. And I told him. To let him know, like."

"Oh, you did, did you? Well, I like the way you let them know. They think I'm going to die. I could see it on my brother's face this afternoon. He thinks I'm going to die."

"I'm very sorry, now, Mr. Chipman."

"Mrs. Kirwen *didn't* say to you I had cancer, did she? She didn't say the doctors had told her something they hadn't told me. Or, did she?"

"Ah, no, sir. Mrs. Kirwen never said you were going to die. 'Tis not Mrs. Kirwen's fault at all. 'Tis my fault, and I'm very sorry now."

"Tell me, Mrs. Leahy. Do you dislike me?"

"Oh, no, sir."

"Then why did you tell these people that I'm going to die?"

"Ah, well, sir, that's a long story. And I'm very sorry to be bringing you news like that. But them doctors don't know everything, now do they?"

"What do you mean?" He was shouting, but he could not stop himself. "Just exactly what the hell do you mean, Mrs. Leahy?"

Mrs. Leahy, avoiding his eye, stared down at her joined hands. "Well, sir, you see, I have something now, something not many people have. And there's times I wish I didn't, let me tell you."

"Didn't what? Didn't have what?"

"I have the sight, sir. The second sight."

"Second sight?" Chipman repeated the words with the joy of a man repeating the punch line of a joke. "Well. And there I was. . . ." Beginning to shake with amusement, he lifted his glass and drank a great swallow of whisky. "You mean you dreamed it, or something like that?"

"Yes, sir. Last Monday, the night before your operation."

"Now let me get this straight," Chipman said. "Mrs. Kirwen told you nothing except what you've told me. The truth is nobody *knows* I have cancer. There's absolutely no proof of it at all."

"That's right, sir."

"My God, do you realize the mischief you've caused?"

"I'm very sorry, now. I see I shouldn't have said anything. I beg your pardon, sir."

"It was a disgraceful thing to do!"

"Yes, sir. I'm sorry, sir. Maybe I should give you my notice?"

"No, no." Chipman poured himself a second drink. Suddenly, he felt like laughing again. "Well, now," he said. Unconsciously, and for the first time in their acquaintance, he found himself slipping into an imitation of her Irish brogue. "And how long have you had this 'sight'?"

"Ah, a long time, now. I noticed it first when I was only fourteen."

"You dream about things and then they happen, is that it?"

"In a way, sir."

"What do you mean. Tell me."

"I'd rather not, now, sir. I'm sorry about speaking to those people. I only meant it for your sake, sir."

"Now, wait. I'm just interested in this premonition of yours. Now, what happened in my case? You had a dream?"

"Yes, just the dream, sir. Nothing else."

"What do you mean, nothing else?"

"Well you see, first there's the dream. And then, later on, you see, there's a second sign."

"And what's this second sign?"

"It's a look I do see on the person's face."

"A look?"

"Yes. When the trouble is very close."

Chipman, in the act of downing his second Scotch, looked at her over the rim of his glass. Ignorant, stupid old creature with her hedgehog eyes and butterfat brogue. Some primitive folk nonsense, typically Irish, he supposed; it was their religion that encouraged these fairy-tales. "When it's close," he said. "What does that mean?"

"When it's close to the time, sir."

"So, I take it you haven't seen this look on my face. Not yet."

"That's right, sir."

"When do you think you'll see it?"

"I don't know that, sir. Better not be asking me things like that. It's no pleasure to me to be seeing the things I do see. That's the God's own truth, sir."

"But how do you know you'll see it? Do you always see it after you have this dream?"

"I'd say so, sir."

"Give me an example."

"Well, I saw it on my own sister, sir, the night before she died. I had a dream and saw her in the dream, and when I woke up she was sleeping in the bed with me and I lit the lamp and looked at her face. I saw it in her face. And the very next night she was killed by a bus on her way home. I was fourteen at the time."

"Tell me about another time."

"Ah, now, what's the use, sir?"

"No, you started this, Mrs. Leahy. I want to hear more."

"And I don't want to tell you, sir."

"But you told Mrs. Kirwen and Mr. Geddes and my nephew. You weren't afraid to tell them this fairy-tale."

"Ah, I didn't tell them that at all, sir. Sure they wouldn't believe it. I just said I had information, I couldn't say more. But that the doctors were very worried about you."

"*Did* you?" Again, he felt furious at her. "How dare you, Mrs. Leahy!"

"I'm sorry, sir. I wanted to be a help to you, sir. I mean I wanted Mrs. Kirwen, and your family and all, to be good to you now in your time of trouble."

I must *not* lose my temper with a servant, Chipman told himself. "All right," he said. "You told me about your sister. Give me another example."

"My husband, sir, God rest his soul. I dreamed about him June second, 1946, and he was took on the second of November, the same year. And on the first of November I saw the look on his face. I begged him not to go to work the next day, but he didn't heed me. He fell off a scaffolding. He never lived to see a priest."

"Wait," Chipman said. "Both these deaths were from accidents, not illnesses."

"Yes, sir."

"Well, have you had any premonitions about deaths from illness?"

"Well, Jimmy, one of the doormen in this building. I saw him in a dream four months before he died of heart disease. And on the day he was taken I went to see him in the hospital. And I saw the look on him."

"Indeed." Slowly, Chipman finished his Scotch.

"Of course, 'tis not always departures. Deaths. Sometimes I do see arrivals. Do you remember, sir, the night you came home from Washington, last New Year's it was? I had your dinner waiting for you. I dreamed the night before that you would come at nine, wanting your dinner. And you did."

As a matter of fact, Chipman thought, I remember it well. I remember thinking she'd prepared that roast lamb for herself and some crony. Extra-sensory perception, premonition: of course all that was only one jump away from teacup reading, table turning, spiritualistic quacks. But she dreamed of my death.

"So, Mrs. Leahy. You dreamed of me, again, the other night. But this time it wasn't about my arrival?"

She nodded.

"Tell me the dream."

"Ah, don't be asking, sir."

"But I am asking. If you go around telling false stories to people about my death, you have the obligation to tell me the truth about what prompted you to do it. Now, what did you see in this dream?"

"I saw the shroud, sir. You came in the room and you were wearing the shroud."

"A shroud. That means death."

"Yes, sir."

"When?"

"Ah, now, I don't know that, sir."

"But you will know, as soon as you see this look on my face, is that it?"

"Yes, sir. I'd know the time, then."

"I see," Chipman said. "And now I suppose you'd like me to cross your palm with silver, so that you'll tell me when I must make my funeral arrangements. Well, Mrs. Leahy, I'm going to disappoint you. A few minutes ago, when I thought of the mischief you've done and the worry you've caused my family and friends, I was quite prepared to let you go. But, believe me, I wouldn't let you go now for all the gold in Fort Knox. A year from now, Mrs. Leahy, you and I will sit here together. We'll have a drink together, this time, this date, one year from now."

"God willing and we will, sir."

He stood up, suddenly feeling his drink, his chair making a screeching noise on the linoleum floor. "And now," he said, "I'd better phone Mrs. Kirwen and those other people and explain what's really happened."

"Yes, sir. I'm very sorry."

He went back into the library. There was no point in being angry with her, it was a joke really. He should be celebrating. The doctors weren't alarmed, and even if they found some malignancy, there are all sorts of treatments, cobalt bombs, chemotherapy and so on. To think that stupid old hedgehog had set all this in motion—Geddes, Buddy, even Geraldine. Poor Geraldine.

He went to his shelves, took down a volume of the *Encyclopaedia Britannica* and read the entry under *cancer*. He then read the entry under *clairvoyance*. When he had finished, he replaced the books and rang the bell.

"Yes, sir."

She stood at the door, her uniform cap on straight, the perfect housekeeper, a treasure, his women friends said. "I'd like some ice and water," he said.

She nodded and smiled. Mrs. Tiggy-winkle. When she came back with the tray, he tried to affect a bantering tone. "Now, just in theory, mind you, just for curiosity's sake. When do you think you'll see that look on my face?"

"I don't know, sir. I hope it will be a long, long time off. Was there anything else, sir?"

"No."

"Good-night, sir."

She bobbed her head in her usual half-curtsey of withdrawal. When she had gone he made himself a fresh drink, then went to the window and stood looking down at Fifth Avenue. People in evening dress were getting out of rental Cadillac limousines in front of his building, laughing and joking, going to some function.

An hour later, he was still standing there. The room behind him was quite dark. He heard no sound in the apartment. He walked into the lighted hallway and went towards the kitchen. She was not there. He went past the kitchen, going towards her room. He stood in front of her door, trembling with excitement. He knocked.

"Yes, sir."

She was sitting in her armchair, stitching the hem of an apron. The television set had been turned off.

"You were waiting for me, weren't you?"

"No, sir. Would you be wanting dinner, sir?"

"You should know I don't want dinner. I thought knowing things like that was one of your specialties."

She bent to her sewing.

"Mrs. Leahy, I want to ask you something. What if I fired you tonight? You'd never see the look, would you?"

"I suppose not, sir."

"Then you'd never know if you'd been right. I mean supposing you never saw my death in the paper. You wouldn't know, would you?"

She bit the edge of her thread.

"Well, answer me."

"Yes, sir, I'd know."

"Look at me!" Even to himself, his voice sounded strange. "You haven't looked at me since I came into the room."

She folded the apron, placed it on the sewing-table and turned around. He went towards her, his face drained. As her eyes met his, he thought again of an animal. An animal does not think: it knows or it does not know. He sat on the edge of a worn sofa, facing her.

"Well?" His voice was hoarse.

"Well what, sir?"

"You know what. Am I still all right?"

"Yes, sir."

"Mrs. Leahy," he said. "You wouldn't lie to me, would you? I mean you'd tell me if you saw it."

"I suppose so, sir. I might be afraid to worry you, though."

His hands gripped hers. "No, no, I want to know. You must tell me. Promise me you'll tell me when the time comes?"

Tears, the unfamiliar tears of dependence, blurred his vision: made the room tremble. Gently, she nodded her head.

P. K. PAGE

THE WOMAN

P. K. Page is best known for her brilliant, imagistic poems—collected in such volumes as The Metal and the Flower, As Ten As Twenty, Cry Ararat!, Poems Selected and New. *But in 1944 she published an extraordinary prose volume of strange, metaphysical fantasy entitled* The Sun and the Moon. *It was republished in 1973 with a number of "Other Fictions", and from that collection we have chosen this curious account of a traveller adrift and the abjectly fearful woman who receives him. It is a tale of loneliness and estrangement that calls to mind lines from one of Page's own poems: "the terrible tourists with their empty eyes /longing to be filled with monuments." Margaret Atwood has noted that Page's prose is that of a poet—strong on atmosphere and mood—and that she creates characters and settings that are "something between nostalgia and horror".*

IN the small villages in the darkness all the square, flat-fronted hotels were shut. Inquiries brought forth the reply that they closed on Sundays. And the traveller? Doomed to a chromium-fitted night in a city; doomed to enter lonely into lobbies where charwomen with mops and brushes worked among palms and ashtrays filled with sand.

No. John renounced the idea with a thrust of his hands on the wheel. No. Already his left arm ached from use and the hand began to float in its own quite isolated climate. At a garage, large, lighted as a night-club, he drew up. The young Frenchman he questioned about rooms ran oil-covered fingers through his hair, leaving a dark mark like a brand upon his forehead. He could phone and ask, he said. As the young man phoned John gazed at the main street. Low hanging lights gathered it in patches to form and shape, released it again to darkness and the feeling of leaves. As far as he could see, the garage alone was bright. There was no challenge here. He must stay.

The Frenchman's voice sounded suddenly loud and reassuring. "*Non, non. Il est très gentil. Très gentil.*"

John realized the man was speaking of him. To someone he had never met he presented a menace. He, John, in his air-force blazer and grey slacks with his damaged arm and bright pink hand.

The Frenchman returned, grinning, nodding, went with him to the car and pointed his finger into the darkness. A great relief enfolded John. He need go no farther. He could sleep. He could lie down near trees. He knew at once that he was very tired. And already he saw the room—the country room of his childhood. Bare boards, wash-basin and pitcher. Slop pail. A window close to the trees.

The woman who opened the door to him stood no higher than the crest on his pocket—dress colourless from many washings, hair colourless from neglect. They stood facing each other in the doorway and he was more at ease than she. She was still afraid.

She stepped back though to let him enter, talked quickly then while she handed him the book and waited for him to sign. He glanced at the names and dates above and saw that he would be alone in the small hotel. He signed his name as she talked, taking his time.

"Before the war, all the time we were busy. Many, many people stayed here all the time. But the business has gone off and now, tonight. . . ."

He barely heard her. And he made no answer. She spoke to release her nervousness. There was no need for him to speak.

She ran up the stairs ahead of him, stopped, beckoning him up. "The room is not ready but—one minute, one minute only." She grabbed his bag with violence as if she wrested a weapon from his hand and ran on again, leading him through a dimly lighted upper hallway with bamboo chairs.

The little room was not as he had seen it but it did look out onto trees—dark masses of leaves and the sound of wind. He stood in the room as she made up the bed, her ridiculously short arms smoothing and stretching, her short legs carrying her quickly from one side to the other.

She ran ahead of him to the bathroom, showing him the way. There she scrubbed and flicked a spotlessly clean basin. He put out his good hand to stop her and she drew away as if burned. So she was still frightened. Very frightened. But would discussing it help her? Were he to say, "I won't hurt you," would it help? He thought not. But he must give her some reassurance. Outside he said, "Good-night, madam—you have taken very good care of me. I am grateful."

Now he sat on the edge of his bed and found it hard. He took off his shoes without bending down, shoving them off with his toes, gazing about him as he did so. The room was very small: a bureau, a wicker table, a bed. That was all. And down the hall from him, probably locked in her room, was his landlady. Why had she taken him in? Why had she not said she was full up? A store adjoined the hotel downstairs and presumably she had existed on it during the war years. Why then, tonight, was it necessary for her to make two dollars? A dozen reasons revolved in his head, followed immediately by one he felt was correct: she needed the experience of change. He remembered the sentence attributed to him as a child, "I'd sooner be frightened to death than bored to death." There were periods in one's life when that was true enough and others—like parts of the war for instance—when the idea of boredom seemed as sweet as a meadow.

He had wiggled his socks off with his toes by now—a trick he'd got into while convalescing. "Don't favour your arm," they had said to him. "You must learn not to favour it." But that was exactly what he did do. The word had horrified him at first, but he had grown to understand it, grown to know its correctness. Despite all their admonitions, he would "favour" it for many years. He removed his blazer and shirt and examined the arm minutely. Not a pretty sight. Quite horrible still, in fact—but—he "favoured" it. He laughed aloud as he stood and stepped out of his trousers.

Then he thought about the woman again and it even crossed his mind that if his guess were true, perhaps he owed it to her to give her a fright. Not a serious one, of course, but something she could talk about afterwards, something which would, for a time, raise her stock among the villagers. It was a pleasant kind of fantasy to indulge in but sleep was gradually overtaking him. The wind in the leaves was a soporific. He switched out the light by the door. The room shrank suddenly with darkness and he walked in a strait-jacket to the bed and lay down. It was good to be lying there, away from the city. He wondered if the woman was asleep. And he slept.

Throughout the night he kept hurting his arm. Pinned between his body and the hard mattress, it would ache and throb and lurch him awake. He imagined himself in the hospital again and listened for the noises of the ward. Then slowly the realization of where he was returned to him. Not in a hospital; not in a city. A small place where there were fewer people to stare. And he would sleep again and awaken hurt, reassure himself, hear the movement of leaves and, once, the sound of feet running on earth—a sound that formed a pattern behind his eyes. But later, towards morning, he walked in a meadow and out through a gate and met himself walking in and the old panic gripped him and he greeted himself with so loud a scream that even when it had wakened him it had not quite completed its length and he heard it still—terrible, like a beast in pain.

And then, very wonderfully, came an answering scream: high, shrill, female. As if he had called to a mate and she had replied with immediate urgency. The sound reached him and fulfilled him and he fell asleep then as easily and completely as if he had had a woman.

Not until the sun burst full upon his face did he waken. And he wakened full of the woman, wanting to see her. For now the idea of her answering scream seemed fantastic to him. If he could see her at once, without delay, he would know.

There were no sounds in the hotel as he dressed. The corridor had a sleeping look—forgotten, abandoned. The bamboo chairs cluttered the upstairs hall. Downstairs the room was bare, shabby and empty. No sign of the woman.

He reclimbed the stairs again in search of her and the half-dozen doors stared mutely in his face. He began knocking on each in turn and as he returned from their silence she emerged from the first he had tried—her face still blurred with sleep, her hands grown woolly overnight fumbling, fumbling with the fastening at her neck.

He knew nothing from her face and he couldn't ask the question. He said, instead, "I would like to pay for my room." And as he extracted the money from his wallet her expression altered. He felt her small eyes hook and sharpen on his "favoured" hand.

WILFRED WATSON

THE LICE

Wilfred Watson has published three books of verse— Friday's Child, The Sorrowful Canadians, *and* I Begin with Counting*—as well as a number of experimental dramas, and collaborated with Marshall McLuhan on a study of the media called* From Cliché to Archetype. *From 1951 until his retirement he taught English at the University of Alberta. In this harrowing tale, he considers the nature of that fascinating human phenomenon, martyrdom—and approaches the subject with an ingenious nastiness that would not have been out of place in the Spanish Inquisition. But then, as his wife, Sheila Watson, wrote in her novel* The Double Hook: *"When you fish for the glory you catch the darkness too."*

1

THERE was a certain bishop of Edmonton who greatly deplored the behaviour of his congregation and of the people of Edmonton, whom he thought guilty of covetousness and greed, envy, sloth, drunkenness, gluttony and lechery, anger, vanity and pride. He would often talk about this matter with his two priests, especially with the younger, whom he loved. But they preferred to think of their congregation as being materialistic. No, no—said the bishop. He liked to call materialism, he said, by its older names. He would roll off on his tongue the Latin terms for the seven deadly sins: *superbia*, *invidia*, *iracundia*, *accidia*, etc. etc. When the people of Edmonton's actions deserved these labels, he wouldn't neglect to apply them, he told his subordinates. That is what these labels were for.

He preached a good many powerful sermons on the subject of the deadly sins. One Lent he preached a series beginning *Pride*, and going on through the list of sins till he got to the last. His congregation took these tongue-lashings in a tolerant way. They—the serious people among them—agreed with their bishop about the nature of sin; but though they felt he was right to preach about the utter holiness of God and the deplorable filthiness of sin, they felt that the bishop didn't rightly understand the tenacious nature of sinfulness. How could he? He was a saintly-minded man, and had mastered his passions and appetites. It was easy for him to resist temptation—and besides, he was a priest, and not only that, getting on in years. He couldn't comprehend how difficult it was for the non-clergy, even when they had a mind to, to cure the sinfulness of Adam in our natures—especially with this demon of materialism attacking us from the radios and television sets, from the newspapers and the motion-picture houses, from magazines, advertising mail and shop windows.

Mr. Dobbs, a good Christian, though heretical on the difficult topic of birth control, said as much to the bishop one day. If only, he ended up by exclaiming, the people of this diocese could be made to *see* their sins—in all their ugliness—as you have described it—then, perhaps, father, then, perhaps. . . .

The bishop thought deeply about what Mr. Dobbs had said to him. . . .

But no way to show his flock the nature of sin came to his mind. . . .

If only sin *could* be made visible.

If only. . . .

At length, he decided to take his difficulty to God.

If only, he said in his heart, God would make the sin of each sinner in the diocese into a hunchback, why, how many souls would be saved for the New Jerusalem, saved in fact from terrible damnation. If only. . . . He shivered a little at the thought. Suppose his own hump were uglier and fatter and more conspicuous than the lump of sin on the backs of his flock? Suppose he himself were, in spiritual pride, uglier and fouler than any of his congregation? It would be for the good of his own soul, he decided, if any condition of sin in him were made manifest.

So the bishop worded an outright prayer, as the spiritual leader of his flock, to God, that the sins of his congregation and of himself should be made visible to himself and to all of them.

Then he fell asleep.

The next morning was Sunday. It was, the bishop saw when he awoke from dreamless sleep, a glorious clear fresh sunny morning. The sun sang in the sky like an angel. The blue sky sang. The trees seemed to be wearing a fresher green than usual, as if they had been washed with rain during the night—perhaps they had—but no—the ground was dry. It was the sun shining through the marvellously clear air of Edmonton that made everything so clean and bright.

In church, when the bishop turned round to look over the new clothes and the clean faces of his congregation, the people themselves seemed newer and brighter and more colourful than ever before. The gay hats of the young girls... the red dresses... the shirts and trousers and jackets of the men... even the blacks of those who had come decently garbed in black... seemed to glow with the colour of the morning and of the sun outside.

A sombre thought struck the bishop. Perhaps there had been another of those false "sales" at the Westmount shopping centre... and this new look... this freshness was simply just that. It was then that the bishop remembered his thoughts about hunchbacks and his prayer to God the night before.

He glanced at the shoulders of his flock to see if his prayer had been—but no, and he said a "Thy will be done" to himself, rather hastily. A terrible fear struck him. He wriggled his shoulders. They seemed, as he did so, rather odd. He squeezed his elbows to his side, trying to feel his back. He looked round, and finally put his hand to his shoulder, as if—and this, he realized glumly, was a deceit, a hypocrisy—he were adjusting his clothing. But no... his terrible prayer... God in his mercy... who sees all issues... had... in his wisdom... seen fit not to grant. *Non sum dignus*....

Introibo ad Altare Dei—Adjutorium nostrum in nomine Domini—I will go into the altar of God—Our help is in the name of the Lord... the bishop had got so far in the saying of the order of mass. And the confession was over, *Confiteor Deo omnipotenti, beatae Mariae semper Virgini*... I confess to almighty God, to blessed Mary ever a virgin.... The bishop had got as far as the absolution: *Misereatur vestri omnipotens Deus, et, dimissis peccatis vestris*... May almighty God have mercy upon you, and forgive you your sins....

It was then that the bishop's eyes fell upon the crucifix on the altar, for at this point he had to turn to the altar and say, silently,

Take away from us our iniquities, we beseech thee....

The words turned to ice in his throat.

For, streaming from the crucifix... was... terrible thing to see, a swarm... yes, swarm of some sort of insects.... No, not streaming from it . . . but drawn to it . . . as if to a magnet . . . which was sucking them in . . . insects. . . .

The bishop didn't know what to think. He wasn't sure what he ought to do. . . . He prostrated himself, burying himself for a time in prayer. . . . Then he stood up before the crucifix . . . and yes . . . it was insects that were hanging in clusters there . . . as if a swarm of bees had alighted . . . as if the blessed crucifix were their queen . . . but, *domine misere*, it was not bees, but some small loathsome insects. . . .

Lice . . . said the bishop. *Lice*. . . . And then, in an instant, the meaning of the miracle—for it was a miracle that his eyes were glazed by—dawned on him, as clearly as if an angel had told him. God had chosen his own way to make the sins of his congregation (and perhaps the sins of the people of Edmonton, too) visible to the eye of sense; he had chosen to turn these foul loathsome wickednesses, evil thoughts, covetousnesses, cupidities of the flesh, into lice polluting the crucifix.

Even when this realization had punctured its way into his mind, the bishop, like someone who has received a telegram of great importance, understands it, but remains unbelieving, put (or rather pushed) forward his arm, and stretched his finger out to touch one of the hideous things. . . . The insect was crushed by the doubting Thomas finger, and a drop of blood smeared—polluted the altar-cloth. Polluted? Ought he, the bishop fearfully checked himself, to conclude, *polluted*? Might not this blood be the blessed blood of the Redeemer of mankind? He sank feebly down upon his knees again, and hid himself in a state between trance and wordless prayer.

Not knowing what they should do, his priests and his acolytes, who had seen almost in the same instant (but with far less comprehension) what he had seen, came towards him, fearing that he had been overcome. But he pulled himself together, and signalled to them to turn to their ritual places.

And he went on, as if instructed by God Himself, in this emergency, with mass. He didn't realize what he was saying. In his mind two ideas were in conflict—swinging backwards and forwards like an irresistible pendulum, which swayed him with its motion. He thought: a miracle, a miracle. But his next thought was: these sins have been turned into *lice*. As far as the glory of the one thought raised him up, the shame of the other sucked him down.

There were hanging to the crucifix, it seemed to him, all sorts of small noxious pestiferous blood-sucking insects. There was the common louse. There were bedbugs, flat and stupid-looking discs of redness; and every sort of louse. He had seen—once, on the farm he was brought up on, a chicken-house hanging with ropes of chicken fleas; and he thought of the pecked rumps of these sorry infected fowl—their featherless backs bleeding where other chickens with no less melancholy backs had beaked them, pecking at lice, but beaking through the skin. But no sight as horrible as the one before his eyes.

When the *credo* was over, he went down to the communion rail, and stood facing his flock. Casting his eye over them, as a shepherd counts his sheep, or as a father casts his eye over his children, he marvelled at their shining faces, at their shining clothes, at their shining presence—the light seemed to come from within them—they seemed like a churchful of angels, not people. The other swing of the pendulum compelled him. He didn't know what to say to them. It certainly wasn't a time for preaching. At last the words came, almost of their own.

"My children, turn round your heads and look at one another."

Surprised, they didn't at once obey him, but stared straight and fixedly at him.

"My children, look at one another."

Shyly, first one and then another turned round to look at his neighbour, and then, catching his neighbour's eye, turned back in a puzzled fashion to the old priest. It seemed to them he stood there in front of them like a shining angel.

"My children," he said over again, with smiling patience, "look at yourselves—turn round and look at yourselves. Take a good look at yourselves. It is a *good* look, isn't it?"

Less shyly this time, they did as they were told, and then turned their eyes back to the priest.

"What is it," he asked them, in the softest voice—in a voice not louder than a whisper—"what is it you see—what do you see? You see," he told them, "the beauty of holiness adorning each one of you."

He stood silent for a long time.

At length he found words to tell what had happened. "God has performed a wonderful miracle. We think in our hearts that there aren't any more miracles performed in this twentieth century after Christ's birth—we think God has lost the ability to do a miracle. But behold, God has performed one. God has shown each of you the beauty of human beings, even in this shape we stand in—it is a beautiful shape, if it isn't made ugly by sin."

He paused. "Look round you at yourselves again." They still didn't understand him, but they looked around about them, as he told them to.

"And now," he said to them, in a voice sepulchral and low—the voice of one buried in the grave, "look at the crucifix on the altar. . . ."

Look at the crucifix on the altar . . . when he said this low-voiced injunction a second time, all their eyes were trained on the crucifix.

None of them could see clearly what it was that had darkened, had clouded over, the shining silver of the cross . . . and the bishop explained to them what had happened. As he spoke, the vision of brightness which he saw resting upon them vanished.

In thrilling fatherly voice he implored them to gaze on the miracle, and see how God had made visible their sins to them, in the form of lice . . . *lice* which he had caused to infest the crucifix, nasty, loathsome, blood-sucking creatures, lice . . . fleas . . . and *bedbugs* . . . and this was why. . . .

His voice trailed away into inaudibility, mere imploration. But everyone in the church understood what he was trying, and unable, to say.

2

When the news of the miracle spread to the world outside—as it very quickly did spread—a nine-days' wonder resulted.

The Edmonton *Journal* gave the miracle front-page headlines, and for several weeks reported daily on the ebb and flow of the swarm of insects to be seen clinging to the cross of the church. *Time* wrote up the miracle in a leading article, honoured the bishop with a cover portrait, and commented on the remarkable reticence he displayed—indeed, complained of it. In truth, he wasn't interested in this sort of fame. *Life* sent photographers to him, but the bishop refused them admittance to the church. Whether they did take photographs surreptitiously, or whether they manufactured them, photographs of the miraculously infested crucifix appeared, in the current issue of *Life*.

Even as far away as Rome, notice was taken of the "miracle of Edmonton", as it was soon called. The Vatican was bound to take an interest in it, for, as may be expected, scientists of a sceptical turn of mind asked to be allowed to test the validity of the alleged miraculous happening. The bishop, however, refused to allow them access to it. They challenged him in the name of truth. There was no lack of witness to the truth, he said. Many eyewitnesses of unimpeachable veracity testified to what had happened—and all that sceptics wanted to do was to find some way of throwing doubt on the occurrence.

The editor of the Edmonton *Journal* held the bishop's stand to be right. An editorial appeared which took the bishop's part against the scientists—this editorial pointed out that the saintliness of the bishop had done more for Edmonton in the way of publicity than anything else in the city's history, with the possible exception of the victories of the town's football team, the Eskimos. To this editorial, a University of Alberta classics professor replied caustically, in a letter, that he, for one, didn't want Edmonton to become another home of superstition, like Lourdes in France.

As for the bishop, he withdrew his skirts with remarkable dexterity from all these unsavoury arguments about what had happened.

His heart indeed was set elsewhere.

And the next Sunday after the appearance of the lice, he rejoiced to notice that the swarm on the crucifix had very noticeably diminished. He might have attributed this lessening (or so I am inclined to think) to a waning of the force of the miracle. But he believed, as a result of their sins being made visible to them, his congregation had been at some pains to resist the temptations of sin; and that the crucifix was a gauge of their success.

When he spoke to them in church, that was what he said. "My children, I rejoice to see that. . . ."

In a low voice, he begged them to try with all their hearts to continue the improvement of the past week. . . he knew that a long-settled-in habit of vice couldn't be cured in a few days. . . but God was helping them. . . and he said he looked forward to the time when the crucifix would be completely free of the lice which still clung to it in swarms. . . .

It is difficult, however, for human beings to resist temptation for periods of longer than a few days, even when all the world has its eye on what is happening; and the second Sunday after the miracle occurred showed a marked increase in the swarming lice.

The bishop in a reproachful voice recalled to his flock what was happening. They looked at his reproachful figure sadly, as if they were all signifying to him, we can't help it, but. . . we are flesh and blood, merely. They received what he said to them in patience, at least. It was not so on the *third* Sunday after the miracle. To the bishop, with anxious eyes on the crucifix of the church as a true gauge of the sinfulness of his people, it seemed, on this third Sunday after God had spoken to them with the plague of lice, as if his flock was more sinful than ever they had been.

His voice, though he tried to modulate it, was petulant. It bit into the air like an iron rasp. He was not heard in patience. People in the church stalls fidgeted and squirmed. It was as if one and all were shrugging their shoulders. When he called on them to look at their shame, visible as lice on the crucifix, they didn't raise their eyes, but looked away almost defiantly. He sensed their hostility.

I must not lose patience with them, he told himself.

Human nature, he reminded himself, is very, very weak. It was natural for his flock to relapse in this way. He must go out to them, as a father, in loving confidence. He stood at the door of his church, after mass, and tried to give each of them his personal assurance of his belief in them. . . .

Person to person, some of them relented of their stiff attitude in church. But others openly rebelled. One of them went so far as to ask, how can we be sure, reverend father, that what has happened to the cross is a sign from God, and not an insult from the devil? Another church member said, was it really a good thing to be able to see one's sins in so dramatic a fashion? He wasn't speaking for himself, mind you, father—but wouldn't it tend to harden people's hearts and make them brazen—just as a prostitute is turned into a brazen huzzy by the outward, open wickedness of her life of vice?

The good bishop shook his head. No, no, he said. We must take it as a miracle from God. If it is a miracle, how can it work for evil?

One of his priests ventured to speak to this question. The younger of the two (the one he loved particularly) observed that, if the result of the manifestation of lice on the crucifix did cause *more* sinfulness, then ought we not to conclude that it was, on this very argument of the bishop, one of the works of the devil?

No, no, no, said the bishop in anguish.

The younger priest held his tongue until the bishop had gone, and then observed, to the other priest, that "we must conclude this, mustn't we?"—"I don't know what to think," said the elder of the two.

The bishop however, received instructions from his superior, the archbishop, that it was plain, from the scandal of the "miracle", that the "miracle" must be adjudged "no miracle". He must therefore have the cross cleansed of the "miraculous" lice, which were, in all probability, due to some natural cause, and to be accounted for as some unusual but perfectly *natural* plague.

This intervention of his superior was perhaps brought

about because some professors of science at the university had examined specimens of the infestation, as they called it, and had pronounced upon the nature of the insects making up their "sample", obtained with a genuine zeal for truth but in an unlawful way. All were such varieties of blood-sucking vermin as could easily be found in Edmonton. There was no satisfactory explanation forthcoming as to how they occurred where they did in such numbers. However, according to one wag, a rough estimate of the number of insects on the crucifix could be made; and hence, a count of the number of sins committed in Edmonton.

Moreover, an analysis of blood taken from some of the lice was made. The reports about this analysis were conflicting. Not all the samples were said to be human blood; and more than one type of human blood was detected. It could not be maintained then that the blood in the lice was the blood of the Saviour, as the bishop was said to suppose. All in all, these investigations didn't completely prove the miracle to be a fraud, but they left considerable room for speculation.

With a sad heart, the bishop ordered the crucifix to be cleansed of the lice infesting it. What his hopes were, may be expected. He was consequently most despondent when, after vigorous disinfection, the cross was once more free of lice.

He went to his room and prayed, not for another miracle, but simply prayed—wordlessly he opened his heart in passive obedience to God. He remained in prayer for most of the night. When the next morning—it was Wednesday morning—he again went into the church, he didn't dare raise his eyes at once to the cross.

When he did so, he saw it was clean—as clean as the cleaning people had left it. He realized that what had occurred might easily be taken as a defilement of the church—that the church might have to be reconsecrated. The archbishop indeed had gently hinted as much in an exchange of letters.

On Thursday, the crucifix was still free of infestation. And so it was on Friday. And on Saturday.

On Saturday morning, the Edmonton *Journal* reported

what had taken place in the church during the week: the cleansing away of the lice infesting the crucifix. Though asserting his belief in the sanctity of the bishop, the editor urged his readers not to draw hasty conclusions from exceptional circumstances. Perhaps this strange happening might prove to be, not a supernatural event, but one of those many natural miracles that our age has provided, and its solution a feather in the cap, not of religion, but of science.

But when, on Sunday morning, the bishop, about to say mass, raised his eyes to the cross, there, lo and behold, were the lice clinging to it, as if it had not been subject to the activities, on the Tuesday before, of the vermin exterminators.

He wanted to cry out, then and there, Look, O ye of little faith, the lice have returned—your sins and mine have again been made visible. But he made no allusion to the repetition of the miracle, as he thought, or to the reinfestation of the crucifix, as most of his congregation thought. He learned that they thought so, as he spoke to them after mass.

They seemed to be daring him to assert that the crawling insect life on the crucifix was, in fact, a miraculous manifestation of their sins.

He held his peace.

By doing so, he earned the approval of his younger priest (the one he loved), who remarked to his brother priest that he thought the bishop had shown wisdom and discretion in maintaining silence in the face of the return of the plague of lice.

The bishop again ordered the exterminators into the church. But Monday, Tuesday, Wednesday, Thursday, Friday, and Saturday—though they exerted all their efforts, the exterminators had no success. They were this time unable to cleanse the cross of its vermin. Nor could they find any natural cause why it should be infested.

They did spray the sanctuary and the body of the church with quantities of an insecticide having deodorant properties. The smell of the lice had become extremely unpleasant—as the younger priest said to his confrère, "God is not only making our sins known to our eyes, but to our noses." The odour of the spray which the vermin-exterminators used rather enforced the stench of the vermin (they seemed unable to kill) than eradicated it or covered it up. As one entered the church, a strong suspicion of violets made one's nose quiver. But this scent of violets quickly changed to a strong whiff of carrion. It was as if, in a flower garden, you were hit by an overpowering smell given off, say, by the putrefying body of a dead animal, a dead cat or dog.

Because of this smell, and for other reasons, I should have thought that there would have been no congregation on the following Sunday, but such was not the case. The fact is, an angry congregation makes a full church.

The bishop, for his part, flatly and without emotion (still calling his flock "my children") reasserted his belief in the miracle. He said that they were right to be ashamed of what had happened to the crucifix, but, though this shame was a good thing, they were wrong to think there was no way to end the pollution of their church.

The church was polluted by sin.

It could be purified by fighting against sin, and God had helped to make this fight easier, by showing them their sins.

The bishop was nevertheless conscious all through mass of the hostility of the people.

After mass, very few spoke to him, but one forthright, golden-hearted old woman spoke out her mind. "I think it is a miracle, father. But it is a very hard one for human flesh and blood to stomach."

"God will provide us with strength."

"It is a very hard thing, reverend father."

3

All that next week, the bishop reflected on what she said to him. He wondered if he had been too fanatical in his zeal to reform his flock. He recalled to mind how he had asked for the miracle, the wonderful vision he had had of his people, that first morning, when the miracle had come, and the unhappy aftermath.

Was God judging *him*? He felt very despondent.

Little by little, however, he began to repair his morale. He chided himself for lacking courage, he blamed himself for lack of faith—he blamed himself, too, for not realizing that he must face a desperate struggle with the forces of evil. He also reminded himself that he had an ally in God.

After all, the bishop told himself, he was the shepherd of his flock, and the good shepherd lays down his life for his sheep. He himself must give up his life for his sheep, if need be.

By Saturday, a course of action shaped itself in his brain. That night, he again prayed articulately to God.

Thy will be done, O Lord—but, if possible, let the pollution of the cross with the sins of my flock cease—even if the lice could infest me—yes, yes, the shame of the polluted cross is too great for them—let the lice infest me. . . .

So he prayed.

The next morning, Sunday morning, he knew that his prayer had been answered, there was no doubt of that. For he himself was covered with the lice. He was torn between thankfulness to God, and the bodily torment of the plague of vermin.

In church, he saw that the cross was free. As he heard mass being said, he began to wonder if he had the strength to undertake the task he had asked for. After the *credo*, he went to the altar rail, and again stood before his flock.

"By miracle," he told them, "it has pleased God to show us all, my children, how our sins hurt His Son. But here is another miracle. He will now show us, such is His will, how His priest is hurt by the sins of His people—your sins, my children."

There was neither joy nor reproach in the bishop's voice. He spoke in a factual manner. Having finished speaking, he divested himself of his clothes, down to the waist. Then he held his arms up above his head, so that all in the church could see how the lice which had clung to the crucifix were now transferred to him.

He walked down the centre aisle of the church and back again, all the time holding his hands above his head.

Then he drew his clothes about him.

He felt, during the rest of that Sunday, and through the other days of the week following, that what God had made happen He had made happen for the best. There was, he believed, a great decrease in the number of lice crawling over his body. He was by no means free from the physical discomfort of them. The comforting thing was, the lice had decreased.

On the following Sunday, he once again experienced the joy he had known, in a surpassing degree, on the day of the first miracle.

It seemed to him that the people in the church were shining with a new cleanness—especially the faces of some of the girls and young women of the congregation seemed to be lit up with the light that must once have shone in the Garden of Eden, the garden of aboriginal innocence. . . .

But, immediately after mass had been said, he sensed a relapse. He knew there must be some retrogression—his experience of human nature told him that. But he suspected from the great increase in the number of lice on his body that the increase had been disappointingly great.

Throughout the following week, the lice on his body increased. In fact, on Sunday, he could hardly bring himself to go to mass.

But he did.

And once again, he stood up before the people, and stripped off his clothes, and showed them his body covered with lice.

"My children," he began, but he got no further.

An unprecedented thing happened.

A woman near him interrupted him. "The smell, father"—this was as far as she got and stopped surprised at herself. "It's the smell of sin—it's your smell, my children," the bishop answered her.

A loud arrogant male voice took up the woman's complaint.

"I'm a Christian, but it's not sanitary for you to appear like this, father . . . you ought not to come into church like it. . . ."

A chorus of voices took up the protest, and soon everybody joined the hubbub.

"You ought to be ashamed of yourself, father, coming to mass like this. . . ." "Stay at home, father, until you are fit to be seen in public. . . ." "This isn't any miracle, father, it's just filth. . . . How can we expect our kids to keep clean and wash the backs of their ears and comb their hair, father, if you come to church all covered with lice?" "Be off with you, father, you're lousy. . . ." "Go and wash, father." "Take a bath, father." "Wash yourself in Lysol, father."

"Shut up," a girl shouted out hysterically.

The bishop steadied himself on the rail of O'Brien's pew, and wrote with his finger in the dust—for the wind had filled the church with the summer dust, which hung over the city like a cloud, and, sifting into the church, made all the woodwork gritty to touch.

A boy's voice whined from the back of the church, "Go delouse yourself in the river Jordan, father."

"My children," the bishop began again, "these are your sins. . . ."

"No, they are lice, father."

"They look like lice, father."

"My children," the bishop wept. . . .

"Off with him."

"Out of the church with him."

"Chase him out."

With the women, girls, and children screaming denunciation or encouragement, the male sheep of the bishop's flock pushed out of their stalls, and, approaching their half-naked shepherd, began to butt him out of the church.

His priests ran to help him into the bishop's residence, which was adjacent. Once in, he threw his discarded clothing across a wooden library table, and then searched in the pocket of his jacket for a packet of cigarettes—it was a packet of Player's he had bought as long ago as the week before the *first* miracle. He hadn't smoked a cigarette since then.

He fumbled with trembling fingers at the packet. Approving this indulgence, one of his priests (the younger one he loved) reached into his own pocket for a booklet of matches, tore off a match, and stood waiting to light the bishop's cigarette. But when the bishop got his box of smokes open, he found the half-filled package swarming with lice. They clung to the cigarette he started to extract, and he pushed it back into the contaminated container.

"Have one of mine, father," urged the younger priest, and offered him a cigarette of his own.

"No, no—no thank you, my son."

"A smoke will do you good, father."

"I will have one of my own," he told his priest. And he extracted the cigarette he had just rejected, tapped it so that the lice clinging to it dropped back into the box, and put the cigarette to his mouth.

The priest lit the cigarette.

But the lice had crept into the tobacco, and the stench of burning insects made the smoking of the cigarette impossible.

The bishop butted it.

As he did so, an upboiling of emotion, a tide burning hot and freezing cold by turns, seethed through every blood vessel, every artery and vein, every capillary, every fibre of his flesh. His skin contracted under its covering of vermin. What he experienced was a recognition. He knew. . . at this moment. . . with absolute certainty. . . that he was picked out to be a martyr. . . and, too, he knew that his suffering. . . the passion of his martyrdom. . . was now begun.

"Lord," he said, "I am afraid. But let Your will be done."

He stood up erect, a sense of glory swelling within him, and pulling at his stiff, slack, aging skin—a sense of glory made trebly delicious to his senses by the itching of the lice which clung to him and were sucking his blood. His skin was aflame. If only the world knew, he thought to himself—it was for nothing so sensually delicious as this, that men lusted after the caresses of harlots, and gave up their immortal souls for the embraces of adultery.

Yet it was an agony.

Embarrassed, awkward, his two priests stood beside him, not knowing what to do, or what to advise. The younger priest was thinking over a course of action. They were both startled when the bishop spoke to them in a voice of command.

"Read to me."

"Read *what* to you, father?"

"Read to me from the scriptures."

"Wouldn't it be better," the younger priest presumed to say, "if you tried taking a shower?—I'm thinking of your personal comfort," he added, for he saw the look kindling in the bishop's eye.

"Read to me from the scriptures," the bishop ordered him.

"Yes, father, what shall I read?"

"From the last chapter of the Book of Isaiah," decided the bishop. *Sion deserta facta est. Jerusalem desolata est . . . quomodo si cui mater blandiatur*—but as one who comforts his mother, I will comfort you. . . .

He understood now, as the younger priest read to him from Isaiah—he grasped now, with the firm-handed grasp of inner comprehension, the meaning of the phrase, *vicarious sacrifice*. He . . . God was going to accept him . . . as a sacrifice for his flock. Because of the shepherd's love for his sheep, the sheep would be saved—what foolish sheep they are! But this, it seemed to the bishop, at this moment, was the most precious of the truths of Christendom. With this imperfect coin of our lives, we can buy the lives of others, and save them from . . . and so perfect ourselves. . . . Yet as he thought these words he realized that he had never loved his congregation. At best, he tolerated them. Indeed, he had *despised* his flock, he had, hadn't he, in trying to purify it—make it what it wasn't? Now he knew the formula. He must offer himself. And God had accepted his pretended love for his people, *as if it had been a real living love*. Or was God showing to him his own worthlessness? No, that was an anthropomorphic idea. Rather, God was taking him at the word of his lips, and overlooking the empty hollowness behind that word—the emptiness of his heart. The bishop recalled the exemplum, the little mediaeval sermon anecdote, of Pers, the usurer. Pers, the usurer, had never done a charitable deed in all his life. But once he had flung, not *in* but *out* of charity, in anger, a loaf of bread at a starving woman. This act of violence had been reckoned—after the system of accounting of heaven—as a good deed to the credit of Pers, the usurer.

"Now let me be for a little while," the bishop said to them, adding, gently, "my sons." He went up to his room. When the younger of the priests visited him after a short lapse of time, he found the bishop collecting together his belongings.

"You are leaving us, father?"

"You have been making arrangements for me to leave you, haven't you, my son?" The apparent clairvoyance of the bishop disturbed the priest.

"Something must be done soon, father."

"Yes, my son. I'm collecting my personal things together. But I shan't, I think, have much use for them."

The priest bowed his head, and left.

4

Later in the day, the bishop agreed, with no fuss, without a single objection, to a proposal of his younger priest. It was that he should leave his see, leave Edmonton, and go into retirement. If he did agree—all the arrangements, said the younger priest, had been made. An unoccupied farmhouse had been put at the bishop's disposal by a member of the congregation, on account of the great scandal the church was suffering. It was provided with bed, table, chest of drawers, other simple furnishings, and the owner wanted no remuneration for it. Nearby, there lived an old woman who had agreed to look after the bishop—she was unfortunately a Presbyterian, but otherwise of unexceptionable character. The arrangement, the younger priest had admitted to the older priest, seemed almost to be a providence of God. "But will he be persuaded . . ." the older man had wondered. "Ah, yes . . . that's our difficulty," said the priest whom the bishop loved. It had proved, however, to be no difficulty at all.

After all the arrangements had been made, there did occur

some difficulty in getting the bishop transported out to his new house. No taxi-cab would agree to accept the lice-ridden churchman as a fare. No one in the bishop's congregation seemed anxious to transport the bishop out there—partly from shame, for no one wanted to be the person chosen to drive the bishop away from the fold; partly, too, there was fear of infesting the car in which the verminous bishop would have to ride.

Put to some pressure, finally one church member offered his car and his services as a driver. It was understood that the car should afterwards be fumigated thoroughly at the church's expense. If the driver of the car picked up any of the vermin on his own person, he too was to be compensated. Some simple precautions were taken. A stout white heavy cotton sheet was draped over the back seat, and another sheet was stretched across between the back seat and the driver's seat—so that the driver would be shielded as much as possible from infestation. Oddly enough, the lice seemed to prefer the bishop to the car or its driver, for none of them (so I was told) were afterwards found either on the driver's person, in the back seat upholstery, in the armrests, in the lining of the car roof, or under the floor-mat. "Isn't that miraculous," the driver said to the younger priest, who had been largely responsible for these arrangements. "Very remarkable," was the answer.

A fairly large crowd gathered at the bishop's house to witness his departure. The police were present, in case of trouble. But there was no demonstration. His farewells were much abbreviated. The elder priest offered to come and live with the bishop. But the bishop, with his eye on the younger priest, whom he loved, wouldn't hear of it. Both priests, he said, were needed in the church. A few intransigents from his congregation assembled a small group of children with fir boughs, which were to have been flung under the car as it drove away. But though the little mites waved their fir boughs faintly at him, no boughs were cast under the front of the car.

The crowd was rather sheepish. They knew the bishop knew they were glad he was leaving. So they merely stood about stupidly. Only one jaundiced teenager called out, with a voice of brass and ashes, "Come back, father, when you've got rid of the lice."

"That will never be," said the bishop, but he spoke to himself merely.

When the bishop had departed, the archbishop from afar caused the church to be reconsecrated, as he had beforehand decided to do.

5

The Presbyterian widow who was to look after the bishop discovered him standing alone in the kitchen of his new house. She had seen his car arrive, and came down "to be of use", she said. She was shocked by the fact that he was unescorted by friends, came, in fact, unaccompanied except for the driver, who, as soon as the bishop had alighted, and his few possessions been put in the house, fled down the road like a juvenile with a stolen car and with a few drinks under his windbreaker. Her good honest Presbyterian heart revolted at what she believed to be the treachery of the bishop's flock. "And they call themselves God's Christians," she exclaimed angrily to herself, "why, I wouldn't treat a dog so. The dirty Catholics. . . ."

She tried to make the bishop feel at home and cared for. But the bishop was not responsive. The woman herself felt strange in his presence, and supposed he must feel strange in hers. As for his affliction, she resolutely closed her eyes to it. She did, however, take pains to assure him that there was a hot bath for him, whenever he wanted to avail himself of it. (The house had propane gas, and the younger priest had arranged to have a new cylinder of gas attached.)

After the bishop had seen where everything was, came introductions.

"What shall I call you, sir?"

"My flock called me 'father'," the bishop told her.

"Very well, sir, 'father' it is from now on."

"And what shall I call you?" the bishop asked her.

"M'name is Mrs. McGinis. You can call me that, if y'like,

sir. But the lads at the ranch, well they call me mom, or mother . . . guess I am older than you, sir, if'n we took a count of our years."

"Then if you wish it—I will call you . . . mother," said the bishop.

"There's some lovely nice hot water in the tank," were her parting words, to which she added, very self-consciously, "father."

"Thank you, thank you," said the bishop.

She went away muttering curses against the Pope, Cardinal Sheen, monsignor the archbishop, and all Roman traitors—"leaving the old man alone, like this. The dir*r*ty Dogans, the dir*r*ty Dogans."

6

All day, the bishop's heart had been anaesthetized by inner misery. But as soon as the Presbyterian widow had left, his feelings began to awake. As long as his heart had been numb, he hadn't noticed the torment of the lice. Now that his heart revived, stirred first of all by the solicitude of Mrs. McGinis, and especially by the flowers she had set out for him at his table, desk, and bedroom altar, he could feel the agony of the lice. He tried to school himself not to scratch at his hands, arms, limbs, or trunk. But every now and again he lost control of his fury, and clawed savagely into his flesh, until the futility of scratching wearied his fingers.

He sat down at the table to eat the meal arranged for him by his part-time housekeeper. But as he reached for the potato salad, cold meats, and pickles that Mrs. McGinis had left him, lice from his body dropped on to the plate of food, and though he tried to brush them away, they seemed viciously intent on getting into his food and contaminating it. At length, he got up from the table without eating. He made tea, but he drank none, for it too was spoiled by lice falling into his cup.

He took off his clothes, because the suffering was less when he was almost naked. He stood up, because the vermin were most bearable in that position.

He was almost caught in half-naked state by Mrs. McGinis, when she called later on in the evening to see if all was well.

After she had gone, he did eat a very little food, and drink a sip of tea. He lay down on his back on his camp-cot, and at long last, very late at night, slept a little. He couldn't pray. All he could do was to keep asking, out of his affliction, *How long, O Lord, how long?*

The next day, he tried taking a bath. But though many of the vermin were drowned in the very hot bath he poured himself, his suffering wasn't lessened, for the water made his skin more tender to the biting of the blood-sucking insects. He couldn't dry himself, because the chafing of the towel set up an intolerable itching. As he stood dripping onto a towel, he decided that bathing was a luxury he couldn't repeat. Anxious not to offend Mrs. McGinis, he was bothered by the state he left the bathtub in. As much as he tried to wipe it clean of vermin, fresh ones fell into it. Finally, he abandoned the task (—an odd fact this, considering that all the reports I have had of the matter suggest that the lice were attracted to him as if to a magnet.)

On the night of the second day, he slept early and long. Next morning, he awoke greatly improved in his mind. He was able to pray; and he prayed for strength. When he had finished his prayers, he encouraged himself by thinking how glorious it was—his terrible fate. He had wanted to cure his sheep of their sins by showing them how ugly they were. But he was doing something better. He was actually helping those who couldn't cleanse themselves. He was taking to himself their iniquity. Certainly not in love—in wilfulness...but...God, he felt sure, was accepting his pitiful effort *as if* it was a true sacrifice. In desperation, he had said, let the sins of my flock come to me *as lice*. It was only half a promise, but God had insisted that he keep it. This was the thought which steadied his heart.

But later that day a relapse occurred. The afternoon was sunny and hot, the humidity in itself trying. He took off his clothes. He tried to pray, but couldn't. He shut himself up in his bedroom and wouldn't see Mrs. McGinis, who nevertheless called out to him, when she left, about the availability of bathwater. . . . And why didn't he take a nice bath? He would feel so much better, she was sure. . . .

Finally, his endurance broke.

O God, he prayed, *let me be rid of these accursed lice, so that I can return to my church. Don't punish me with them any more. I've had enough. O God, let me be set free of this torment.*

He fell into a long sleep.

In the morning, all the lice were gone.

7

He couldn't at first believe either his eyes or his skin, over which he kept running his finger. He immediately threw himself into a great tub of water, and bathed himself with wonderful enjoyment. He was amazed to find that his skin was completely rid of irritation. He gave himself a marvellously revitalizing rub-down with the bath towel. He shaved, a thing he hadn't been able to do. Then, feeling like a new man, he had an excellent breakfast, drank two cups of instant coffee, and smoked three or four cigarettes.

When Mrs. McGinis came about eleven o'clock in the morning, she said to him, "Why, father, you look as if you'd taken on a new lease on life!—I see you've had a bath," she added, glancing in at the damp towels in the bathroom. "I told you it was all that was needed—it's the simple remedies that work. Nothing like soap and water. You see," she told him, "you have another nice hot bath tonight. Keep them at bay it will."

She insisted on changing his bedsheets. "But—why, you haven't soiled them at all," she said.

The next morning he took another bath.

He wondered how long he ought to wait before going back to his church. A day—or two days? He seemed so useless, just waiting around in the farmhouse. He smoked cigarettes, given to him by the younger priest as a farewell gift. He ate his meals.

He thought of how surprised his congregation would be, to see him again, so quickly. There would be no reproaches. It might be that he would love them better than he had done hitherto, because of the bond of failure between them—he had failed and they had failed. There would be mutual forgiveness. As he conceded his failure, as, putting it on like a new garment, he got somewhat more used to it, his need for the *community* of the church became more insistent. He must get back right away.

But at the end of the day, he discovered one thing: he *could never go back*. It would require just as much courage of him, to think out the new philosophy of life going back would require . . . the excuses . . . the new goals . . . that. . . . Ah, just as much . . . as staying.

That night he didn't sleep at all. By morning, he found himself, with his new vitality, hating his cleanness. He bathed himself contemptuously. If only, he said to himself, I still had the lice—better the torment of the lice, than the emptiness of what I am now.

He didn't dare pray.

But, by that evening, he could endure himself no longer. *O God*, he prayed, *let the lice return to me. Forgive my weakness. Let the lice return, if it is Your will, let the lice return . . . non sum dignus, domine, sed. . . .*

He fell asleep. When he awoke, it was morning. The lice had returned. They were much worse than before.

8

So much worse were they, that before the evening of that day was come, he had again prayed that the lice leave him. In the morning, he was again free of them. He couldn't hesitate now—he mustn't play fast and loose like this. He packed his handbag. He prepared to leave. He would go back and love his flock, this would be the meaning of all that had happened . . . for him and for them, for they in return would love him too.

But when he was ready to leave, his decision wavered again. He unpacked his clothes, he decided to stay. He paced up and down the farmhouse, into and out of all the rooms of it, like a caged tigress, her cubs taken from her and her dugs full of milk. He saw that he couldn't live in this state of irresolution, but it was a long time before he could once again bring himself to pray. It was early the next morning before he could pray. But then, a little before two-thirty a.m., he was able to. *Let the lice return to me. Let the lice return to me*. He then slept for an hour or two. When he awoke, they had come back. Back, and much worse than they had been on their second return. He took off his night-clothes and lay for a long time naked on his bed.

The lice seemed to be multiplying. They were gnawing in his arm-pits—he tried to clean them out. If he rested on his back, they crawled across his belly. They crawled across the small of his back, if he lay on his belly. They got into his groin, and into his ears—he had already put wads of cotton wool into his ears, to keep the lice out, but they worked their way past that barrier. Into his ears. What lies, the thought shrieked across his brain, are my people breeding now? The vermin crawled into his anus. They crawled across his scrotum, and got into the folds of the *glans penis*. What sodomy are they now committing, he cried out, as he scratched at his rectum . . . what fornication or prostitution or pimping or adultery am I suffering for now? The lice crawled over his hands—cupidity, cupidity, he told himself. . . .

They crawled into his navel—across his teats—into his eyes—into his mouth, even. . . .

When Mrs. McGinis called promptly at eleven a.m., she found him completely naked. But it wasn't his nakedness that horrified her, it was the sight of the true deformity of his condition, which, till now, had been more or less hidden from her. Good honest woman that she was, she shrieked with terrified disgust, when she saw *that*. All her fear of him turned into vituperation and reproach. "Why don't you do as I told you?" She threw the bathroom door open.

"Do as I tell you," she screamed. "Get in there and bathe yourself until you are clean again."

He shook his head piteously.

"Look, father. You're going to obey me. Into that bath."

He shook his head.

"Goddam you," she shouted, "do as I say."

When she found that he wouldn't or couldn't do as she ordered him, she banged her fist down on the table. "Very well, father. Very well. If you won't take steps to cure yourself, it's the last you'll see of me. Good-day. Good-day." She slammed the door, and went muttering to herself up the path.

The bishop knelt down to pray. *Lord, have mercy upon me*, he murmured . . . *but, O God, if I pray to be free of the lice . . . and I will pray to be free of them . . . have mercy upon me . . . don't ever listen to my prayer. Don't ever listen to my prayer. Let the lice be with me*. When he had said this prayer, he felt, for a moment of bliss, as if this resolution had carried him up into the seventh heaven of paradise . . . as if his martyrdom was completed.

He was able to say the Lord's Prayer, and to make a brief act of contrition. *My God I love Thee*.

But then the torment started again. He kept shrieking, take the lice away, take the lice away, take the lice away. Then he would stop from sheer exhaustion. And then one thought would gnaw in his brain: what is the use of it? Isn't it all entirely useless, like mountain-climbing, aren't I like the mountain-climber, who only keeps on to get to the top, because he has engaged himself to get to the top? Again the bishop would moan, take the lice away, take the lice away. Then again his outcry would exhaust itself, and he would think, I'm like the anaconda serpent which has swallowed too large a deer and can't let go of it because inward-curving snake-teeth have trapped both the snake and the victim. He was, the bishop told himself, the snake, and God, the deer. He couldn't spit God out, if he wanted to. He also thought, these lice will purify me, but how can they help my flock, how? They continue as they were. Then once again the bishop would begin to keen, take the lice away, take the lice away, take the lice away. . . .

Then his mind could think no more. He could only rage. Far across in the McGinis ranchhouse, they could hear him roaring. Mrs. McGinis put in a call to Edmonton, but could get no one at the church. When, however, the next morning, there was complete silence, the good woman again telephoned, and asked that someone be sent to the bishop's assistance... because... she was afraid of the worst....

9

It was at the eleventh hour that the bishop gave up the ghost. His friends, summoned on the next day, did not arrive at the farmhouse until the next morning after that. They saw then a third miracle, if the lice on the crucifix were considered as one miracle, and the lice on the bishop himself, another. What they saw was, out of the mattress of the camp-cot, a thick turf of a marvellously green new grass growing. On, or rather in, this grass, were the remains of the bishop. All the lice were gone, and only his skeleton was seen, at first. There was absolutely no sign of any vermin, no flea, no bedbug, no louse of any kind.

Summoned by the Presbyterian-minded Mrs. McGinis, it was the police who made a second discovery. One was a constable and the other a corporal. The constable *observed* that death couldn't have been recent. The corporal, however, *looking* more closely at the bishop's remains, saw that, within the bony cage of the churchman's ribs, the heart and other chest organs were still fresh and new.

At this, the clergy were filled with fear, for they knew what had happened *must* be a miracle. "I'm afraid," said the constable to the corporal, "there has been foul play."

These policemen were to be present at the performance of yet another miracle.

The first to discover the bones, the younger priest (whom the bishop loved in particular), when he perceived what had happened, drew back. He didn't want to look at the miracle. It was there. He was convinced that it had happened. But there was nothing inside him to receive it. I am like a barren woman, he thought. The bridegroom comes into me, and I don't conceive. He smiled to himself, thinking what would a psychologist make of a celibate Roman Catholic priest using such imagery? He went into the bathroom. When he had made water, he put his hand to the hot-water tank. It was, of course, warm. Then he went into the kitchen, and there he saw the carton of cigarettes, which he had given the bishop as a parting gift. He saw how many the bishop had smoked. And thinking of what he had *done* for the bishop (for besides the cigarettes he had out of his own pocket arranged to have the cylinder of gas attached, so that there could be hot water always available for the bishop's use), he was ashamed of *how little* he had done.

Pushing his way through the others who were still wondering at the bishop's remains, and pushing aside the policemen, who speculated as to the possibility of a crime, he flung himself down before the bishop, seized the bishop's hand, and wept, Forgive me, father.

It was then that the final miracle occurred, before the very eyes of the police. A great swarm of vermin appeared to descend upon the bishop's heart, as if to devour it.

Seeing this, the younger priest fainted away. When he had been carried into the kitchen, laid on the floor, and restoratives given, someone of the party noticed that the lice had consumed the bishop's remaining vitals, and that the skeleton was now completely free of the organs inside it.

But when they looked for lice, there were none to be found.

MICHEL TREMBLAY

THE THIRTEENTH WIFE OF BARON KLUGG

It took Michel Tremblay three years to find a producer for his first play, Les Belles-Soeurs, *but when the curtain finally went up he was famous overnight. He has since written such popular plays as* Forever Yours, Marie-Lou, Hosanna, *and* Bonjour là, bonjour. *His reputation as Quebec's leading contemporary playwright has eclipsed his earlier début as a writer of weird fiction; his first publication was* Contes pour buveurs attardés, *a collection of twenty-five macabre stories (translated by Michael Bullock under the title* Tales for Late-Night Drinkers). *The story which follows, from that collection, strikingly combines a Gothic theme, a modern style, and a fascination with the inescapable Bluebeard.*

"KARLA von Kleiber, do you take this man to be your wedded husband?" How tapering his fingers were! ". . . do you take Karla von Kleiber to be your wedded wife?" And how powerful his hands were! "May God bless your union. . . . " But why was it taking so long? "Karla, just think. There have already been twelve Baroness Kluggs." Why shouldn't she die right away? "They all disappeared under strange circumstances." Air! Air! "Will you take this woman . . . this woman. . . ." Oh, how long his fingers were. "I love him so much, Mother. He is so kind to me." Life would not leave her body. "But he may be a criminal, my daughter." Life refused to leave her body.

And then. . . .

At last! At last! It was coming. Death was there.

And it was gentle, like fainting.

When it was all over, Baron Klugg put the portrait back in its place and calmly went off to bed.

The Baroness was afraid.

When he had approached her, when he had put his lips to her forehead, when he had caressed the nape of her neck with his gentle hands, the Baroness had seen nothing.

But when he had turned around to look at her before leaving his wife's bedroom, the Baroness had seen. Yes, she had seen that ferocious look, that inhuman look that wished to disfigure her. The Baroness had felt that her husband wished to rend her face with his eyes.

She had bolted her bedroom door and had left a nightlight burning when she went to bed. In the middle of the night, at the hour when the big owl in the garden went hunting, the Baroness had heard a sound in the corridor.

She was certain that she was not dreaming. And she was afraid.

Nevertheless, now, in the middle of this ball, her husband was beside her and he was joking as he held her arm. Her husband who, the night before. . . .

The Baroness was afraid.

There was a sound of muffled footsteps. Of footsteps someone was muffling. Who was walking about in the corridor like that in the middle of the night? A bird outside had uttered a cry of distress and the big owl had flown past the window laughing. The Baroness had risen and gone to the door.

But whom could she ask help from at this ball? All these people were afraid of Baron Klugg. That was well known. No one would dare. . . .

The footsteps had stopped outside the door of her bedroom. For a long time she had listened, with her ear glued to the door. But nothing moved any more. And yet there was the sound of breathing. He was there.

Baron Klugg turned to his wife. "What's the matter, Karla? You seem thoughtful."

"Nothing, my friend, nothing—a migraine."

"Would you rather go home straight away?"

"No, no! I'd rather stay here."

Baron Klugg raised his eyebrows. She had spoken these words in such a strange tone. Could she suspect. . . .

Suddenly, just beside her head, the doorknob had started to turn. Slowly. The Baroness had watched the doorknob turning, and the time it had taken to make a half turn had seemed to her so long, so long.

The Baroness was afraid.

The Baroness was trembling.

"Are you cold, Karla?"

"Yes, a little."

He helped her to put her shawl round her shoulders and slipped his arm round her waist. But was his caress not a little too abrupt? Was he not squeezing her waist a little too tight?

"You're hurting me."

The Count and Countess Mirmf laughed.

She had been sure she heard him swear when he realized that the door was bolted. Baron Klugg had sworn when he realized that his wife's bedroom door was bolted.

The nightingale had uttered its last cry of distress and the owl had stopped laughing. He was gravely devouring his prey, scrutinizing the night with his huge eyes.

Baron Klugg had gone away. The Baroness had wept. Not that she was sad; but she was beginning to believe that what people said about her husband was right.

She would so much have liked to ask help from someone. But from whom? Feigning a slight attack of giddiness, she asked the Baron and the Count to excuse her, and she took the Countess Mirmf with her.

"It's true," the latter said when they were away from the others. "It's true that you don't look well. Is something the matter?"

"Do you know anyone in the police?" asked Baroness Klugg suddenly.

"What? The police? My dear, we don't have anything to do with those people."

And she went off and told everyone that Baroness Klugg wanted to meet people in the police.

But instead of laughing, people looked at the Baron and Baroness in an odd way. "There's another one," they said, "another one who will disappear in strange circumstances. But she is the first who dared to utter the word police. She will pay for her audacity, poor thing."

The Baron and Baroness Klugg left the ball a few minutes later, the Baron having found his wife very much changed, very pale, suddenly.

She did not want to go back to the castle. She did not want to be alone with her husband. She did not want to go back to the castle. She didn't know what awaited her, but something told her not to return to the castle. Never again. Or else she would never leave it again. Never. Never again.

"You are thoughtful, Karla."

The Baroness had cried out.

"And far too much on edge."

The coach was definitely going too fast.

"I can't ask the coachman to go slower, Karla, I'm in a great hurry. I have something to show you."

They came to the castle.

How loathsome this castle was in the dark! The Baroness had never liked these homecomings from balls: she didn't like to see her husband's castle in the night. All those square towers, all those closed, dark windows, all those doors shut and abandoned for years made her shudder. How sinister was the castle that sheltered Baron and Baroness Klugg. And the Baroness Klugg was her. Karla. Karla was her name. Karla von Kleiber, the Baroness Klugg.

Her head was spinning.

"The Baroness Klugg disappeared mysteriously last night. Karla von Kleiber, the thirteenth Baroness Klugg, went to join the twelve others in the tomb. An inquiry has begun."

"You're not listening to me, my dear."

The Baroness jumped and noticed that they were inside the castle.

The Baron came up to her and took her in his arms.

"You're trembling. Are you afraid?"

She said she was cold.

All around the hall, the Baron Klugg's first twelve wives were looking at her and smiling with their fixed smiles. The Baroness stepped forward to look at them all, each in her turn. They all had long fair hair, blue eyes, and a long neck. They all looked like her. She had already noticed that, but it was only now that this frightened her.

She felt her husband was watching her. Perhaps with the same expression as yesterday evening.

She turned round abruptly.

The Baron was no longer there.

She stood still in the middle of the hall. Alone with the twelve pictures of dead women who were looking at her with a smile. And yet she had the clear impression that her husband, too, was watching her. She felt that her husband was spying on her, hidden behind a pillar or a curtain. She dared not move. Suddenly she remembered that the Baron had told her he had something to show her. Her heart contracted still further.

At the same moment the lights in the hall went out.

The Baroness felt something brush against her hand and she cried out.

She heard a sliding sound. As though someone were dragging something very heavy across the floor. A sliding sound. Like a body being dragged along. Perhaps it was her body. Already. Already she felt that her body was being dragged along and put down. . . .

In the darkest corner of the room, where the blackness was most opaque, was thickest, the sliding sound stopped. A faint light made a hole in the darkness. Just a tiny little hole. A little hole of light in the black sea of the darkness. An insignificant little hole. A shivering, grubby little hole that moved from left to right, up and down.

Baroness Klugg, her eyes wide open, made her way slowly towards this light.

A whisper.

"Come, I have something to show you. Come, Karla, come here. Closer. Closer. Come, Karla von Kleiber, thirteenth Baroness Klugg, come here. Closer. Again. Closer."

It was dark. Baroness Klugg stretched out her arms in front of her to avoid knocking into the furniture. When she was quite close to the little light, her hands touched something wet, stretched out vertically in front of her. The Baroness quickly withdrew her hands and wiped them on her dress.

Then a dozen other lights joined the first and Baroness Klugg saw her husband beside her, a big candlestick in his hand, smiling at her. "Look," said the Baron, "I've painted your portrait."

Two paces in front of her stood an enormous portrait. A long white dress. One hand resting on the dress. The other on the back of a chair. A portrait in every respect like the twelve others. A fixed smile. In every respect like the twelve others.

And that expression! That expression in the blue eyes that seemed to be calling for help!

The portrait was still quite fresh.

"I have painted your portrait," repeated Baron Klugg.

The Baroness's hands were smeared with paint and she wiped them on her dress.

Baron Klugg put the candlestick down on the floor.

He took Karla by the hand and drew her away from the portrait.

"Look," he said. "See how like you they are. See how like them you are."

A candlestick was burning beneath each of the twelve pictures and at the end of the series of portraits the Baroness saw a hole in the wall.

"That's where I'm going to put your body," whispered her husband.

While fear froze the Baroness's heart, Baron Klugg went up to the first picture in the series and pressed one of its corners. The picture moved aside without a sound.

Everything began to spin around Karla. She closed her eyes and put her hands to her throat. She opened her mouth to scream, but she could not utter a sound. Behind the picture, nailed to the wall and covered by a long white dress, the skeleton of the first Baroness Klugg was laughing silently. When she opened her eyes, the twelve pictures had been moved to one side and twelve skeletons were looking at her and laughing. A suffocating odour of decay filled the room.

"You already look like them," murmured Baron Klugg.

All the candles went out and the Baroness began to run.

LAWRENCE MATHEWS

THE DEATH OF ARTHUR RIMBAUD

Arthur Rimbaud, the French poet? He's dead, of course. Everyone knows he died in France in 1891—Or did he . . . ?

Lawrence Mathews teaches English at the University of Alberta in Edmonton. His stories and poems have appeared in a number of literary magazines, and in 1977 he published a volume of poetry, The Sweet Tears of the Judge, *which includes these lines from "The Kitchen at Midnight":*

If I open these curtains,
I will see my face
reflected in the glass.
Beyond that,
the darkness begins.

IT came as quite a surprise to us, to learn that it was Arthur Rimbaud, the famous poet, who'd rented the old farmhouse on the other side of the river. He'd been here for several months before we found out, and then it was only by accident. One of the kids at the high school—it was Dave Hutchinson, Bill's son—came across the name in some book in the school library, probably the *Encylopaedia Britannica*. He pointed it out to Dick Delacroix, the French teacher. Delacroix had never heard of any poet named Rimbaud, but he did some checking, and soon we had the whole story. Rimbaud himself had never said a word about it.

Of course, some of the details were hard to swallow. For one thing, Rimbaud the poet was supposed to have been born in 1854, which would make him well over a hundred, but our Rimbaud didn't look a day over thirty-five. Then there was the fact that the poet was supposed to have had his right leg amputated, and the Rimbaud we knew had both legs. And the poet was supposed to have died in 1891. When the story about the name started going around, most of us more or less suspended judgement.

None of us knew Rimbaud too well, although he seemed a pleasant enough person. We didn't see much of him at all. Even though the farmhouse he lived in was only two miles or so up the road, he never came into town more than once a week. (He used to drive a pick-up truck, an old blue Chev.) At first we thought maybe he didn't trust the old covered bridge that crosses the river. It's perfectly safe, but every time you drive across, it feels like it's going to collapse, and sometimes strangers are pretty leery of it. Finally one week somebody asked him if that was it, and he said no, that didn't bother him at all, it was just that he liked his privacy. He was like that. He never volunteered any information, but if you asked him, he'd tell you without hesitating. Not that anybody asked him much. We believe in minding our own business here. Even so, when we saw him buying his supplies or driving off in his truck, we couldn't help but wonder what he was doing out in the farmhouse, all by himself, week after week.

He made it clear right from the start that he didn't want to be bothered. I think it was November when he moved in, around the time of the first snow. Anyway, at the end of the month, Harry Graves, his landlord, drove out to collect the rent. Harry was a bit annoyed when he found the gate padlocked. He had to climb over it and walk the hundred or so yards to the house. He said later that Rimbaud was polite, but obviously not too happy to see him. When Harry asked him about the lock, Rimbaud said he was worried about prowlers, which was ridiculous. We don't have problems like that around here, and anyway, there's hardly ever any traffic on that road.

Harry said he explained all this very carefully, but Rimbaud didn't really seem to be listening. The other thing that put him off, he said, was that Rimbaud kept him standing in the hallway instead of inviting him in. From what Harry could see of the front parlour, it looked like it'd been turned into a chemistry lab. There were wooden benches Rimbaud had apparently made himself, with fancy pieces of equipment made of metal and plastic. Bunsen burners, test-tubes filled with strange-looking liquids. There was a funny smell about the place too, Harry said. Rimbaud was quite evasive about the whole thing. He said he was doing some research of some kind, for a book he was going to write. Harry let it go at that. Afterwards, Rimbaud made arrangements to leave his rent money at the post office, so Harry wouldn't have to drive out to the farmhouse.

On Saturday afternoons, Rimbaud used to stop at the British Arms for a few glasses of beer before driving home. The time after the story about his being a famous poet had become common knowledge, some of us invited him over to sit at our table. He seemed a bit reluctant—nobody'd ever asked him to drink with them before, not out of hostility but because he seemed to prefer it that way. But he did come over. It was Baxter Martin who asked him, point-blank, if he was Arthur Rimbaud, the great poet. Rimbaud said yes, he was, without batting an eyelash. He seemed to loosen up a bit after that, at least compared to what he'd been like before.

Before long we'd asked him the other questions that had been bothering us. Baxter said what about being born in 1854, and Rimbaud said that at the age of thirty-five or so, he'd just stopped aging, it was as simple as that. There were reasons for it, but he couldn't go into them now. He also said both the amputation of his leg and his death in 1891 had been faked, something he did because of an insurance policy he wanted his mother to collect on. He'd felt badly about it at the time, he explained, because he didn't like to be deceitful. But he knew by then he wasn't going to age any more, and his mother had a life-insurance policy on him, one with double indemnity in the event of loss of limb before death. He wouldn't have done it if she hadn't needed the money badly.

Clyde Dunbar, who's an insurance agent himself, said he'd never heard of a policy like that. You could see the hurt look in Rimbaud's eyes. But then Baxter asked Clyde sarcastically if he'd made a study of life-insurance in nineteenth-century France, and Clyde said, well, no, he hadn't, and Rimbaud brightened up again. In a few minutes, he excused himself, saying he had things to do at home. After he'd left, Steve Adams remarked that he had an honest face. Nobody disagreed.

Life in this town wasn't quite the same after that. You have to understand that nothing much has ever really happened here. No famous explorer ever passed through this part of the country. There have been no battles, no acts of heroism, nothing we can look back to with a lot of civic pride. It hasn't been any different in this century. The industries are farming and lumbering. People grow up, work, raise families. We've never had a boy win the Victoria Cross or make it in the NHL, or a girl who became a movie star or had quintuplets. The only local political issue is the bridge, and that's pretty dull. Even though we know the old covered bridge is safe, most of us think we should have a new one, something that looks half-way modern. A lot of politicians have made promises about it, but nothing ever gets done. But when you come down to it, probably nobody really cares that much about the bridge—it gives us something to argue about, and that's as far as our interest in the subject goes.

So when the Rimbaud thing came along, it had quite an impact. Not in the commercial sense: it was only Joe Summers, the proprietor of the British Arms, who thought of making money out of it. And his plan to build a motel to accommodate visiting Rimbaud enthusiasts didn't come to anything. The rest of us never thought in those terms at all. Instead we started to get excited about the poetry itself. It didn't take long. Dick Delacroix was the first enthusiast. He had a friend in the city send up a volume of Rimbaud, and reading it was like a conversion for him. He could hardly talk about anything else. The funny thing was, the people he talked to got just as enthusiastic, without having read a line themselves. Interest started to snowball. Jack Watson at the drugstore ordered fifty copies of the paperback edition of English translations, and they were sold out in two hours, even though everyone knew you didn't get the full flavour with a translation. Before long the school board had Delacroix giving night extension courses in French so people could get their Rimbaud in the original.

Once the courses got going, people talked of nothing else but Rimbaud's poems. You couldn't go into the British Arms without getting into an argument about the meaning of "Voyelles". For a while Baxter Martin and Clyde Dunbar weren't speaking to each other because Baxter followed the alchemical interpretation and Clyde believed the visual dimension was more important. People you met in the street would quote bits of *Une Saison en Enfer*, and you'd be expected to know what came next. But I guess "Le Bateau Ivre" was the favourite. Horace Warner, the United Church minister, wrote an article for the *Herald* to prove the St. Lawrence was one of the "*fleuves impassibles*", and after that we thought of it as "our" poem. Miss

Zanini's fourth-grade class chanted the whole thing at the school concert, and everybody said it was the highlight of the show.

The odd thing was, Rimbaud himself never took any interest in any of this. He knew what was going on, of course. When he came into the British Arms on Saturday afternoons, people would come over to his table and start firing questions. Mostly they'd want him to explain a particular line or image. He was usually polite, but you could tell he found the whole thing pretty tedious. Finally, one Saturday, Steve Adams asked him if he would say, in a sentence or two, what the main thrust of his *oeuvre* was, and Rimbaud just got up and walked out without answering.

After that, he stopped coming in to drink. He'd do his shopping as quickly as possible and head straight home, not speaking to anyone he didn't have to. A few weeks later, matters came to a head. Young Dave Hutchinson, the high-school kid who'd started the whole thing, stopped Rimbaud in the street and asked him to autograph a copy of the Penguin edition of the *Collected Poems*. Rimbaud said sure, he'd be happy to, as long as he didn't have to answer any questions. But as he handed the book back, he said, quite distinctly, "Listen, kid, I think you should know it's all a pile of shit." Several bystanders heard it.

That upset a lot of people. What sort of man would make a remark like that about great poetry? An interest in Rimbaud's biography blossomed overnight. New controversies erupted. There was the drug thing, for instance. Steve Adams said it was proof positive Rimbaud was a degenerate. But Clyde Dunbar said anybody could make a mistake (his son had received a suspended sentence for possession the year before), and anyway there was no evidence that Rimbaud still used drugs. Then there was the thing about his running guns for the Arabs. That put a few people off. But then somebody down at the Legion pointed out that it wasn't all that different from what Buzz Beurling had done after the war. Rimbaud still had his defenders, but a lot of us were asking questions. And then there were mysteries. What about the "lost years", as we called them now, between 1891 and the day he arrived in our town driving his Chevy pick-up? How did he get into the country? And what was he doing out in Harry Graves's farmhouse, with all that chemistry equipment?

It was Baxter Martin's idea to invite him to be guest speaker at the next Rotary Club meeting. Baxter thought it would be a way of clearing the air, as he put it. Everybody agreed it would be a good thing. When Rimbaud came into town the next Saturday, Baxter was waiting for him. "We used to think you were going to fit in here," Baxter said. "Now we're not so sure." Rimbaud just stood silently while Baxter explained about the Rotary meeting, and how a lot of people thought Rimbaud had a funny attitude, and this would be a chance for him to explain himself. The Poet thought it over for a minute or two, and then said all right, he'd do it.

Everybody wanted to come. Joe Summers filled the banquet room at the British Arms with as many extra tables and chairs as he could get, and there were still people standing in the back. That atmosphere was tense. Not that anybody was expecting trouble, just that we knew the whole question of Rimbaud's status in our community was going to be settled once and for all, one way or the other. Baxter was the chairman, as usual. Wanting to be fair, he gave Rimbaud a big build-up: "a great poet, a man who needs no introduction . . . a figure of controversy in recent weeks", and so on. Nobody really listened. We were all staring at Rimbaud, who seemed completely at ease, even slightly bored. Then he was walking up to the mike. There wasn't much applause.

We weren't prepared for the speech he made. I guess we thought he'd give us some sort of explanation as to why he'd been so indifferent to our interest in his poetry. Maybe he'd include some defence of his character regarding the drugs and the gun-running. Most of all, we wanted him to say that he hadn't meant it, when he'd said that his poetry was a pile of shit. But what we got was something quite different. He started by saying he understood that we had been puzzled by his behaviour, but that he wasn't going to try to justify it. Instead, he wanted to demonstrate his desire to be a good citizen. He paused to take a sip of water, and then announced his intention to run as an independent candidate in the next federal election.

All over the room, people started talking. There was some laughter, but most of us saw immediately that the idea had merit. Our town is off in the corner of a large, mostly rural, constituency. We've never had an MP come from here. But once word got around that Rimbaud was world-famous, a great poet, and that electing him would focus national attention on our constituency and its problems, we knew he'd win easily. And once he was in, at last we'd have a member who would be committed to doing something for our town. Of course, we don't need that much. And we're not greedy. But federal money would have been nice. And maybe Rimbaud could finally have done something about getting us our new bridge, through some federal-provincial cost-sharing programme, or some outright grant for out-of-the-way areas — there must be plenty of ways to do things like that.

All these things were going through our minds in the two or three minutes it took Baxter to restore order. I guess Rimbaud's popularity had never been greater than it was at that moment. When he tried to speak again, he was stopped several times by cheering, until people began to realize what he was trying to say. He had begun to present his programme, the programme he said he would "work to have implemented". I can't remember all of it, in fact different people have different versions of what they heard him say.

Later on, when we tried to piece it all together, everybody had a particular detail they remembered best. One, for example, was that Bay Street should be given back to the Indians. There should be statues of Tim Buck in all shopping plazas. The armed forces should be sent to Antarctica on a permanent peacekeeping mission. The RCMP should investigate the underground activities of the IODE. The anniversary of the Winnipeg General Strike should be made a national holiday. "The Cremation of Sam McGee" should provide the lyrics for a new national anthem. Louis Riel should be given an unconditional pardon. Stephen Truscott should be made Minister of Justice. Ukrainian should be made an official language, with immersion courses in all kindergartens. Our borders with Quebec should be abolished. If we put this programme into effect, he said, we would soon be ready to annex the United States. There was more, but that gives you an idea.

It was very quiet when he stopped. There was no clapping, of course, but no boos or hisses, either. Someone at the back did shout "Communist!" but nobody took it up. Still, everyone knew Rimbaud was through in this town. People started to leave, and Baxter didn't bother to go through the formality of thanking the speaker. Rimbaud, as I recall, went back to his chair and sat down as coolly as he'd got up in the first place. He stared off into space, as though completely unconscious of the effect he'd had.

Public opinion crystallized quickly. For the next two days, people talked of nothing else. That week's *Herald* had a front-page editorial about "undesirable elements in our midst" whose "red political philosophy conflicts with the democratic system." There were several angry letters to the editor, too. But it was Horace Warner, in his Sunday sermon, who came up with the only practical idea, and we adopted it enthusiastically.

It was only a couple of weeks before Dominion Day. (I know they've given it a new name now, but we still like the old one.) Warner's idea was that the Boy Scouts should go around town collecting every volume of Rimbaud's poetry that hadn't already been thrown out. On the first of July, they could bring the books down to Mackenzie King Park, by the river, where the fireworks display was to be held. As a kind of grand finale to the programme, we could have a bookburning, the first in the town's history. Besides releasing a lot of pent-up emotion, Warner reasoned, the bookburning would also serve as a very pointed hint to Rimbaud himself about the town's new attitude towards him. The plan was endorsed by the town council at a special meeting on Monday.

Dominion Day came, and everything went according to plan, but the bookburning turned out to be a bit of a flop. There just weren't enough books to make a very impressive pile, and a small bonfire is bound to be an anticlimax after a fireworks display. Maybe we should have had it earlier in the evening. Or maybe Warner's idea wasn't such a good one after all. When it was all over, some of us didn't feel like going home.

We sat on the riverbank, drinking straight rye out of paper cups. It was a hot night. We stared at the moonlit water, not saying much. (The river has an Indian name, hard for outsiders to pronounce—we hardly ever use it ourselves.) We were all thinking about Rimbaud, though nobody mentioned him at first. He hadn't come into town since the day of the speech. His supplies must have been running pretty low. Harry Graves had gone out to give him his month's notice. He said Rimbaud was outside working with his chemistry equipment, apparently dismantling it. They had a very short conversation. Rimbaud hadn't said where he would go next. When Harry told him about the bookburning, he hadn't seemed surprised. "He acted like he didn't give a shit," Harry'd told us. We thought about this as we watched the water flowing towards the old covered bridge. Rimbaud had come here and made fools of us, and now he was getting ready to walk away. We didn't like it. It wasn't long before we ran out of rye.

I think it was Baxter Martin who finally said, "Let's get the bastard." It could have been Joe Summers. Probably it doesn't matter. There were twelve of us, we took three cars. Crossing the bridge was like going through a dark tunnel, and we all felt that familiar shaky feeling, as if the whole structure was about to collapse, and then we were through, and driving a dangerous fifty along the two-mile stretch of dirt road that led to the Graves farmhouse.

The funny thing was, Rimbaud was waiting for us, right at the gate. He must have heard the cars coming from a fair distance. Maybe he'd guessed who was coming and why. But then why didn't he try to get away in the truck? Or if he thought we might have cut him off, why didn't he make a run for it, across the fields? He had a fair chance to escape. Anyway, there he was. It was so unexpected that when the headlights picked him up, I thought at first it was an animal that had strayed down from the hills. But that only lasted for a split second, and then I saw it was Rimbaud, in his black leather jacket. He was even smiling, faintly.

It didn't take long, and I guess the details aren't important. There was no record of the death. In a town this size, it's not too difficult to keep things quiet, if everybody cooperates.

ANDREAS SCHROEDER

THE LATE MAN

"I can write to my heart's content about madness and the strangeness of the world by looking at what's right in front of my nose. I can make use of that in a way that makes it realistic in the sense that it's believable to people, but not at the same time necessarily realistic writing. It all depends on what you choose to see. . . ." So wrote Andreas Schroeder, who grew up in a Mennonite community in British Columbia and began writing as a child in reaction to his isolation and his confusion about the outside world. He has published several volumes of poetry, a collection of short fiction called The Late Man, *and a prison memoir,* Shaking It Rough.

ON the morning after the storm, the fishermen got up earlier than usual to survey the damage and repair what could be saved. Unusually strong winds and rain had scattered the nets and flattened gardens, bushes, even trees. Fishing-boats lay strewn about the beach like broken teeth. Everywhere an exhausted silence hung limply; even the occasional sea-gull screech seemed blunted and uncertain. Across the mud-flats the faint rush of breakers seemed to fade, though the tide was coming in, slowly and without apparent conviction.

At this time in the morning the fishermen rarely spoke. They arranged their lines, oiled pulleys, checked over their engines, and wordlessly pushed out to sea. To break the fragile silence of the first few hours would have been like bursting a delicate membrane without preparation; it was tacitly understood that a man needed more time to clear away in his mind the rubble and destruction of the preceding night, than was available to him between his getting up and the launching of his boat. Even after they had cleared the beach and set their course for the large fishing-grounds farther north, the fishermen rarely raised their voices—as if in instinctive respect for the precariousness of the human mind launched before sunrise on an uncertain sea.

But someone broke the silence that morning; as the last remaining boats poled into deeper water to lower their engines, a young bearded fisherman pointed to a single unattended boat lying on its side on the beach and asked in a low voice: "Where's he?"

The man being addressed looked startled, puzzled, then shrugged his shoulders.

The bearded fisherman risked a further offence. "Could he be sick, d'you think?"

There was no response. The other man slid his oar into the water and pushed them off.

A man opens his cabin door and steps into view. He is the late man, the man whose boat lies untouched on the beach below his cabin. There is nothing particularly unusual about this man except perhaps a certain slight hesitance in his manner; the hesitance of a man for whom the world became at some point intensely suspect, for whom, at that point, a glass on a table became less and less a glass on a table and more and more a thing too strange and amazing to grasp by name. As he stands in his doorway, his hand rests gingerly on the frame, as if constantly ready in case of attack.

About fifteen minutes have passed since the last boat was launched and the late man stepped from his cabin. Now, his boat ready and his outboard spluttering half-submerged, he pushes off and follows the fleet towards the fishing-grounds.

A few hours later the fishing village begins to yawn, stretch, and get up; children and fishwives clutter the streets and tangle the air with punctuation marks.

When they return in the early evening and pull their boats out of the water above the high-tide markers, the late man is not with them. During the interval of time between the last fisherman's ascent from his stranded boat to his waiting dinner and the late man's arrival at the launching site fifteen minutes later, silence holds the breach like an indrawn breath. The sound of his prow on the pebbles, therefore, grates in an unusually harsh way on the nerves of the woman waiting for him above the high-tide markers. He has caught fewer fish than the other fishermen.

The next morning the late man appears at his cabin door half an hour after the fisherman have left the beach. Their boats are already vague in the distance when he finally manages to haul his boat to the water-line, which has by this time fallen far below his landing-place with the receding tide. He seems somehow weakened, older, leaning wearily against the wheel of his boat. When the fishermen return that night he is an uncertain speck on the horizon, half an hour behind the last of the fishing fleet, and when the catch is scored, he has caught fewer fish than the day before.

Around noon the following day the boats were anchored in clusters to share both lunch and small talk on the fishing-grounds, and the conversation turned to the late man. "Can't figure 'im out," one fisherman mused, pulling thoughtfully at his beard. "Won't tell nobody what's wrong." "Ain't sayin' a thing," another agreed. "Asked him yesterday what the problem was, but I'll be damned if he didn't seem like he wasn't even listening." There was a pause as if to let the spoken words disperse. Then: "Sea can do that to a man. Catches up with him, it does." The speaker slowly shook his head, threw an orange peel overboard, then absently ignored a deck-hand who had asked him what he meant. The deck-hand finally turned away, assuming his question was naive; he was new in the fleet and often found himself going unanswered. As it was, he was already on the other side of the boat when the old man muttered his answer to no one in particular: "I don't know what happens; I just know it does. Ain't no man can whirl the world by hand."

The next morning the late man launched his boat some forty-five minutes after the fleet had left the beach.

Little is known of the late man's history, though this is not realized until he first begins to attract attention by his mystifying dislocation of schedule; suddenly everyone rummages about in their memory for initial impressions, former opinions, latent suspicions, old predictions. Little in the way of substantial information is collected. It is generally agreed that he is a relatively young man, hard-working and "well-disciplined". Some felt him to be a little too much given to reflection, but one suspects this is said chiefly in reaction to his if not exactly antisocial, at least fairly reticent manner. He cares little for other people, though he has been known to go to the aid of a complete stranger for no reason. A slightly more observant villager notes his peculiar tendency to touch (with a curiously disbelieving air) whatever happens to be around him; the remark is received in uncertain silence. Many frankly admit they have no idea what to make of the whole business, and that the man is probably simply under the attack of some unsettling virus. This fails to explain, however (as someone quickly points out), his consistent, almost plan-like deceleration of pace in relation to the normal fishing schedule of the village—by this time he is reported leaving the beach a full three hours after the last of the other boats has been launched.

By the time the late man pulls his boat from the water, the sun is little more than an almost-submerged leer on a mindless horizon and the waves have jelled to heavy, slowly swirling jibes. Night winds begin to cover the eastern part of the sky with a thick, cumulous ceiling of ridicule. Sardonic chuckles ripple along the water-line where the undertow pursues an endless foreplay with beach gravel. The late man stands motionless, looking strangely as if he belongs neither to the water nor to the land; his face is a ploughed field but his eyes dart about the beach like frightened piranhas. His boat is a crazily tilted sneer lying on its side in the pebbles, with rope dangling from the prow like corded spittle. Wave upon wave of curling laughter lampoons the beach. Everywhere, everything grins. The late man no longer defends himself. He has committed the blunder of allowing himself and the universe to discover his detective activities, his secret investigations into the nature and composition of himself and whatever he finds it possible to apprehend. But he has allowed this discovery prematurely, before he has had time to properly anaesthetize his specimens, and now, suddenly aware of a spy in their midst, they have disintegrated into countless labyrinthine possibilities and traps and the late man is cut off without the possibility of retreat. He has long since given up trying to sledge-hammer his brain to sleep.

But a violated universe will not be satisfied with the simple deflection of an inquisitive mind, and as if to make certain that such a trespassing will never again be possible, it has turned glaring spotlights against the late man's brain, blinding and overwhelming it with confusion and derision. Stiffly aligned principles and corollaries suddenly go limp and begin to collapse; endless qualifications overrun simple premises and leave behind a shambles of tattered and useless shreds of belief. Above all, the horror is set creeping up the back stairs of the late man's mind that all this is beyond his control, and that like a retaining pin pulled from a spring-loaded wheel, this destruction will continue relentlessly until it has unrolled the tension from the spring.

There appears to be little he can do but to hold on until all is done, and to hope that he does not become so weakened in the process as to fall prey to a useless madness.

In a matter of months the departures and arrivals of the late man and the fishing fleet have diverged to such an extent that the returning fishermen see the late man's boat heading towards them at dusk, on its way north towards open water. He stands huddled over his wheel, eyes staring unseeing at the darkening horizon as if in purposeful blindness. The fishing fleet parts to let him pass; though no one appears to understand, everyone sees the desperate undertow in his eyes and says nothing. When all the boats are secured and the gear locked away, the late man is a dissolving blotch against black evening. A few moments later he is gone.

The late man had returned the previous morning with no fish at all.

As he sat down to dinner, the young fisherman who had asked about the late man early one morning suddenly spoke of him to his wife. "Nobody knows anything, or they won't say anything. Everybody pretends to ignore him. I've got to find out."

His wife said nothing. He looked at her curiously, then threw down his knife. "Well damn it, here's a man digging his own grave in plain view of a whole fishing village, and nobody has the guts to look into the matter." His wife remained silent but a worried look began to unsettle her face. The young fisherman stood up abruptly. "I'm going to find out," he said, reaching for his squall-jacket and opening the door. "Even if for no other reason than a simple matter of self-defence!" he added as the door slammed shut. Footsteps receded from the cabin. Within minutes the sound of his outboard began to move across the bay towards the fishing-grounds and the open sea.

For a time the young fisherman directs his boat through thick total darkness; a bulging cloud cover muffles the moon and the night sways and sidesteps in ponderous movements that are blind but everywhere. The occasional clear splash falls short among the sluggish gurgle and sagging cough of deep-water waves beneath the keel. The young fisherman peers at the bleakness but steers his boat by instinct.

As he moves farther and farther into deeper water the night begins to thin out; his eyes detect edges, outlines, occasional glimpses of phosphoric glitter—eventually the moon disentangles from the clouds and trudges high into the sky, spraying a fine shower of thin light over the fishing-grounds. By this time the young fisherman can make out the dark shape of the late man's boat, lying at anchor on his starboard side. The booms on the boat before him are out, trailing thin glistening lines into the water. The late man is fishing.

The young fisherman sits unmoving at his wheel, uncertain as to what should follow. Possibilities dart in and out of his mind, unwilling to bite. He waits, his brain idling slowly, his thoughts loose.

A creak from a rusty tackle interrupts the silence. A glass-float dips and scrambles; the late man comes alive and begins to reel it in. A strike.

The young fisherman straightens up and strains to see. The glass-float tugs and splashes at the end of a stiff line; the late man's figure curves against the mast, his arms taut like two rigid claws shaking with exertion. The young fisherman feels an instinctive excitement thrill through his body as if the strike were his own. Something huge is on the end of that line.

The glass-float is almost at boat's edge, momentarily calmer. The late man reaches for his fish-net and plunges it over the side, scooping carefully. His back is turned to the young fisherman, obscuring the float as he brings it to the boat's side. The fish-net rises from the water, then stops.

Surprised, the young fisherman leans forward but sees only the hunched back of the late man leaning over his net. A fierce rippling movement shakes the arm holding the handle as somethings twists and writhes in the meshes, but the late man makes no move to pull it into the boat. Ten minutes pass; the late man still stands bent over his net, gazing at his catch. The young fisherman is unable to see his face.

Finally, in a slow but deliberate movement, the late man empties his net into the sea and straightens up.

The young fisherman watches, still dumbfounded, as the late man repeats the same procedure moments later when another line snaps alive. This time his demeanour seems to indicate recognition or less interest; a short look suffices to make him empty the net again. After a short pause a third float begins to bob and the late man reels it in. Half an hour later he is still engrossed in the net's contents, ignoring all the other lines which are jerking at the boom. Bent over the gunwale, his hair blowing about his head like spray in the wind, the man stares at his catch in silence, then throws it back into the sea.

As a faint paleness begins to tinge the outermost edges of the dark, the young fisherman stands up stiffly, a nervous flutter in his stomach, strangely excited yet uncertain why. He detects traces of the intoxication of discovery in his feelings, though he has no idea what he has discovered or realized.

Carefully pulling out his oars, he mounts them in the oar-locks and prepares to slip away. By the time the sun appears he will be back in the bay and his cabin. Then there will be time to think.

A small sound from the other boat stops his raised oars short. The late man has emptied his net and stepped back towards the mast. As he half-turns to reapply bait to one of the lines the young fisherman catches a glimpse of the late man's face. He almost drops his oars.

The late man's face is totally disfigured. Crumbled skin, twitching lips, and bleached white hair, he is suddenly old—an uncertain fool barely able to hold his balance in the rocking boat. The young fisherman is stunned. The late man was of the same generation as the others in the fishing fleet—chronologically about thirty years old. Now he looks three times that age.

But there is no time to lose; the horizon is becoming a thin pencil-line of light across the dark and he will be discovered. Stealthily moving his oars, the young fisherman pulls away towards the south and the fishing village.

As his boat moves into the bay, he sees the first cabin doors opening and fishermen walking down the beach towards their boats. Several of them look up, surprised to see his incoming boat at such an odd time. Obviously his wife has said nothing. He steers towards an unused part of the beach and runs his boat aground.

There, his boat bouncing slightly to the rhythm of his fading wash, he sat on the bow and twisted a piece of rope between his fingers; uncertain, almost nervous, uncertain again. The spreading sun warmed his back as he sat, but his stomach remained cold and unsettled; he felt the desperate urge to run, to commit a violence, tear something to shreds, but somehow he was numbed or simply unable to move. For no apparent reason something seemed to have snapped; his senses coiled and bunched in twisting knots, thoughts whirled in ever-tightening circles about his head, and a steadily mounting pressure threatened to explode inside him like a surfacing deep-water fish.

Then the faint growl from a distant engine punctured the silence and the tension drained away with an almost audible hiss. The young fisherman looked over his shoulder and watched the late man's boat increase towards the bay. Several of the other fishermen paused and shaded their eyes. For a short while everything hung in suspension. . . .

Suddenly the late man's boat is in the bay, its engine silent, drifting towards the beach. As its prow gouges into the sand the late man struggles feebly to climb off the deck onto the gravel, half-falling several times in the process. Then hoisting the bow rope over his shoulder, he attempts to pull his boat higher up onto the beach.

Later, after the late man had been buried and the fishermen had returned to their boats, the young fisherman was heard to say that in a totally paralysed landscape, the only moving thing had been the late man trying to beach his boat. They had watched him for an incredibly long time, trying to raise the bow above the gravel, and when he finally collapsed, still no one had moved. When they eventually began to climb down towards the fallen figure, the landscape seemed to stretch and expand in every direction and they walked for hours before reaching him. They found him lying on his back, his face contorted with a mixture of agony and amazement; it was the oldest face they had ever seen. So they had buried him, quietly and without looking at each other, and the young fisherman had beached the boat. The next morning, due possibly to the tiring events of the preceding night and day, the young fisherman slept a little longer, and eventually launched his boat some fifteen minutes after the last of the fishing-boats had cleared the bay.

ETHEL WILSON

MR. SLEEPWALKER

Ethel Wilson (1890-1980) wrote novels and stories of great sensitivity and understanding, set in an urbane, whimsical world in which perfectly reasonable, well-mannered people—like Mary Manly, in the story you are about to read—suddenly find themselves faced with situations that are absurd, outrageous, even surreal. Mrs. Wilson began as a Vancouver school-teacher and doctor's wife, and was nearly sixty before she published her first novel, Hetty Dorval, *in 1947. She soon followed that with* The Innocent Traveller, The Equations of Love, Swamp Angel, Love and Salt Water, *and a short-story collection,* Mrs. Golightly and Other Stories.

DURING the time that Mary Manly's husband was in Australia, Mrs. Manly had an experience that was peculiar. I should like to say that up to the time that her husband went to the war, Mrs. Manly had never shown any tendency to undue imagination, nervousness, hysteria, nor to any of those weaknesses which are supposed to be the prerogative of her sex, but are not —any of which might have been considered responsible for the mounting episodes which culminated in her nearly killing Mr. Sleepwalker. Let us begin with Mary Manly, because we do not know very much about the past of Mr. Sleepwalker. It would be provocative, but not fair, to speculate about Mr. Sleepwalker's past, but, unless we knew something about his origin and his history, the speculations would be useless, and disturbing.

Mary Davidson married Hugh Manly who was a forester in the government service of British Columbia, and so able a man was Hugh Manly in the matter of conservation of forests, marketing of lumber—especially as these things applied to the province of British Columbia whose forests are among her noblest treasures—that his government began to send him on long journeys to foreign countries where export trade might be developed, and it became no great surprise—but a source of something like grief—to Mary when Hugh walked in for dinner, and said later on in the evening as he often did, "Well, it looks as though I'm off again," and Mary would learn that Hugh was being sent by his government to South Africa, or to the United Kingdom, or to Sweden, and so it was that Mary had to gear herself—as they say—to these absences which became to her a mounting sorrow, because she loved her husband beyond expression, and he loved only her. Each time that Hugh left he said something like this, "Next time, darling, we'll see if you can't come too," and Mary would say, "Yes, next time,

Hugh." But next time Hugh might go to Hyderabad, and how can a young wife whimsically accompany her husband to Hyderabad, when there is a future to look to? I mention all this because it is possible that the unhappiness of repeated separation, in a world whose essential limit is bounded by the life and love of two people closely united, may have done something to Mary's otherwise calm and extroverted nature, and may have made her susceptible to outside influence of an esoteric, suprahuman, or even subhuman kind.

Just at the time when it seemed that Hugh had approached the point in his chosen profession at which he could say, "Come with me and be damned to everything and hang the expense," there came the war. Hugh went to the war, and Mary's sense of separation became exacerbated to the point where it was anguish. Are we who love each other so dearly, she said to herself, always to be deprived of our greatest joy, and have I to accustom myself to the theory that we belong to each other *in absentia* only, for it is an actual fact that the woman in the next apartment and I have lived for seven years with only one wall dividing us, and we do not belong to each other; while Hugh and I, who belong to each other, have lived for seven years with half the world between us most of the time. And now this war!

She busied herself at once, but in spite of being daily involved in responsibility and detail, her other life—that is to say, her absent life with Hugh—gradually became more real to her than the life of meetings, administration, billeting, in which her body was engaged, especially after Hugh left for overseas. ("Onlie the body's busy, and pretends.") Again I say that this other-worldness, which developed in Mary, and in many other young women like her during those years, but more in Mary Manly, because absence and frustration had already made some mark on her before the war began, may have been responsible for many queer things, one way and another. Directly the war was over, Hugh came home (fortunately) and was placed at once at the head of his department; and before the two had spent a month together, Hugh was sent to Australia. "You're coming this time, Mary, and no nonsense about it," said Hugh, and Mary with rapture prepared to go, broke her left elbow, and Hugh went without her.

To go now to Mr. Sleepwalker.

Before Hugh went overseas he was stationed for a while in Winnipeg. Mary camp-followed him to Winnipeg, and it was in Winnipeg that she first saw Mr. Sleepwalker. It was in a streetcar. The streetcar swinging along Portage Avenue was full, and Mary stood, holding onto a strap. She looked idly about her, and the swaying of the streetcar so determined that her eyes fell upon this person and that sitting in the row of seats immediately beside the entrance to the streetcar. She saw a small slim man sitting in this seat, with people on either side of him. Mary's whole attention was taken by this man, although no one else seemed to observe him, and as the body of someone swaying beside her interposed between her and the small man seated, she did not see him, and then she saw him again.

She became violently curious about the small man, and began to speculate about him. He appeared unaware of people around him, and certainly unaware of Mary's scrutiny. If I were accustomed to menservants, thought Mary, or if we lived in a different age, I should think that this little man is, or has been, a "gentleman's gentleman". He is drilled in some precision of thought and action, and he hides behind that soft and deferential pose and immobility some definite and different entity. The small man sat erect, looking straight ahead of him, servile yet proud, his hands—in worn black gloves—folded on the head of his walking-stick which rested between his knees. His hat was a kind of square obsolete bowler. He wore a wing collar, and a small black tie of the kind known as a string tie. His black suit was old, worn, and very neat. Below the anachronistic hat was the face that so attracted and repelled Mary Manly. The features were neat and of a prissy femininity. The eyes were a warm stealthy reddish brown. His hair descended in reddish brown sideburns; otherwise he was clean-shaven. The hair was soft and unlike the hair of a man; in fact it resembled a soft fur. His mouth was set—so, with gentility. He is a mixture, thought Mary, as she watched the little man, now and again obscured from her, of gentility—a fake product of civilization—and of something feral, I do not know what. I seem to have seen those russet eyes, she continued to herself, in some animal. Is it a fox? No, I know no more about foxes than about gentlemen's gentlemen, and yet it seems like a fox. Or a watching hawk. Or some red-eyed rodent. And why is he in the middle of Canada, in Winnipeg, new city of grain, utility, and railroads, looking like this, dressed like this? He is as much a phenomenon in his dreadful respectability, riding on an unlikely streetcar in the city of Winnipeg, as if he wore a crown, or a grey topper, or a sarong. What life does he lead, and why is he here? The small man sat alone, it appeared, in his personal and genteel world, politely apart from those who rubbed shoulders with him or crowded his neatly brushed worn buttoned boots, and he looked straight ahead of him. Mary now avoided looking at the small man, because, so lively had been her interest in his peculiarities, she was afraid that he might become aware of her, and she did not want this to happen; so she turned her back, and faced in the other direction. Then she got off the streetcar and, for the moment, forgot him.

On the next evening, Hugh came in from barracks, and they had dinner together. Mary tried to tell Hugh about the small man on the streetcar, but found that she was unable to describe him in such a way as would interest Hugh; and when Hugh told her, as he did, that he was ordered east and that he thought that embarkation would be the next step, this drove other thoughts from Mary's mind and she determined at once to move east also, because, as she said, "We may as well continue living together, Hugh, in our own peculiar haphazard fashion. I have really loved it in Winnipeg, and who knows but that they may keep you in the east longer than you think. So I shall not go back to Vancouver. I shall go east, too." Mary then prepared to go east, following Hugh, who left at a day's notice.

She had by this time attained (she thought) a fairly philosophic regard for things as they have to be, realizing of course that she was only one of the millions of persons—friends and enemies—whose lives were dislocated by war; that she could expect no special privilege because she was Mary Manly, wife of Hugh Manly (usually *in absentia*); and that she could and must assume the matter-of-factness which is necessary in the successful conduct of life, which other people achieve so admirably, and which passes very well for courage. So she took life as it came, allowing herself to hope, as was natural, that her husband would be kept in Canada, although a part of each of them wished that he would be sent away and would see action, but safely, with everybody else, and no favours sought or granted. Mary said good-bye to her friends in Winnipeg, many of whom, like herself, were also in motion one way or another, and then, late one night, she boarded the eastbound train.

Because Mary was what is called a good train traveller, she soon bestowed her things neatly away and settled down for the remainder of the night in her lower berth. She slept at once, and only in a half-conscious and comfortable way was she aware of the stopping, starting, moaning, creaking of the great train. Suddenly she was awakened by a quiet. The train was standing still, perhaps in a siding, because there seemed to be no noise, or it may have been in the night-time stillness of the railway station of a town. Mary was half awake, and did not care. She was sleepily aware of stillness, of time and place suspended—and then of persons passing quietly, almost stealthily, in the aisle outside her curtain...the porter...perhaps...passenger...porter...a murmur...a smell...earth...rotted wood...an animal...in the sleeping-car...impossible...a smell...earth...rotted wood...an animal...it passed. She fell asleep.

When day broke, the train had left Manitoba and was speeding into the vast western wooded lake-strewn regions of Ontario. The train stopped at Chapleau for twenty minutes. Mary got out, and wandered, as she always did at Chapleau station, to the small stone memorial that bears the name of Louis Hémon. Why, she wondered, did Louis Hémon come to Canada, write his book which, although unknown to most young Canadians, had already dimmed to a reputation faintly classic, and die? And why did Louis Hémon die, still young, at

Chapleau, straggling rawly beside its railway station and its forests? A young man stood beside her and studied the carved words. Mary looked up at him and spoke tentatively. "Do you know why Louis Hémon came here?" she asked.

"Sawry," said the young man awkwardly, "I never heard of him. I was kinda wondering myself who he was," and he strolled away.

Mary turned and walked briskly up and down the platform, with the breeze and against the breeze that blew refreshingly through Chapleau. She heard the cry "All aboard." She turned towards her own porter at her own car. As she waited to mount the steps, she saw walking down the platform the small man in black whom she had seen in the Winnipeg streetcar. She was startled to see the small figure in motion. He walked, one might say, with as much stillness as he sat, regarding no one. He walked with his arms at his sides, guarded, genteel, like a black-suited doll. She climbed on the train, entered her car, and found her seat. She did not see him again.

When she rejoined Hugh in Halifax, there were many urgent things to think about without recalling to mind the small man whose hair was like fur, and so it seemed that he had never been. Hugh's convoy sailed, and Mary Manly went back to Vancouver and put herself at once to work.

It was months later that Mary Manly and Thérèse Leduc went to a movie together. At the end of the first picture, the two people who were sitting beside Mary went out, and, in the dark, another occupant took the seat beside her. Suddenly Mary's attention was taken from the screen by the scent, slight at first, then stronger, of, perhaps, an animal, or, perhaps, rotted wood, thick and dank (but how could it be rotted wood?). This smell was not at first heavy, but pervasive, and was very unpleasant to her. It became at last heavy in the air, and made her uneasy. It recalled to her a journey. . . a what? . . . some smell . . . not train smell . . . something that passed by. She tried to look at the person next to her without appearing to do so. This was difficult. She murmured to Thérèse Leduc, "Do you smell anything queer?"

"No," whispered Thérèse. "What kind of thing?"

"I don't know," answered Mary.

"I smell nothing," said Thérèse.

The smell persisted. Suddenly the skin on the back of Mary's neck seemed to prickle. The man (it was a man) who sat beside her was small, and sat very still. Mary sat still too, and thought, "I want to get up and leave. I can't. That is unreasonable." But at last she whispered to Thérèse, "I'm sorry, Terry, but the man beside me *does* smell. Let's get out . . . perhaps we can move. Let's go your way."

The two women got up and shuffled out of the long end of the row.

"How disgusting!" expostulated Thérèse.

"Yes, wasn't it? It really *was*," said Mary, but she did not explain that the smell was not what Terry thought it was. Not dirt. Nothing like dirt. Something animal. Something wild. They found other seats, but Mary could not give her attention to the play. After the movie, she discovered also that she could not tell Thérèse about the small man, and about this animal smell which she had begun to associate with him. The thing was fanciful, and Mary did not like to be thought fanciful. Most of all, she did not like to admit to herself that she was fanciful. But there it was. She put her mind to other things, and that was not very difficult.

Some time later, as Mary rose from her knees in church, she did not need to look in order to see who it was that had come into the pew and had now dropped on his knees beside her. The feral scent wafted and then hung heavy. The small man in black drew himself up to his seat, and sat, doll-like, prim, just as (Mary knew) she had seen him sit in the streetcar on Portage Avenue. She saw him as plainly now as though her physical eyes observed the genteel shape, the russet fur of the sideburns, the prissy set of the mouth. He sat beside her, she knew, correct, genteel, yet vulpine, if it was vulpine. Mary's head began to spin. My imagination plays tricks, or does it? she asked herself. . . . Soon, of course, I shall see the two people in front of me move, turn slightly, disturbed by the smell that disturbs me. It cannot be to me, me alone, that it comes. He carries it round with him. Others *must* smell it—always. He is horrible, horrible. But now I can't leave... I must stay... he can never have observed me (for we never think, do we, that we are the observed ones; always we are the observers), I shall sit here. I shall stay for the service, and outstay him. But he is horrible. And a revulsion at the proximity of this small being almost overcame her, and she felt faint.

The little man sat still; his worn-gloved hands were on his knees, she could see. He took his Prayer Book and found his place, following the service respectfully, and in an accustomed manner. Mary's mind worked obliquely, directed, in spite of herself, towards the small man.

But the two people in front of her did not turn round, disturbed by the alien smell of rotted wood, of something animal, unknown.

Mary outsat the service. Then, with elaborate negligence, while the small man was leaving and after he had left, she put on her gloves, leaned back in her pew, and awaited the end of the slowly drifting columns of church-goers moving with slightly rocking inhibited motion down the aisles. Then she joined the departing stream at its end, went out into the open air, felt refreshed and, by a foolishly roundabout way, returned home.

I shall tell Hugh, she thought. It's very silly. I take this too seriously, and if I tell Hugh, I'll get rid of it. The thing bothers me out of all proportion. What concerns me is the war, and Hugh, and my jobs of work to do, and my life that I have always had; and a small being that smells like—perhaps—a weasel or a musk-rat has no part and does not matter. So she wrote, but when she read the letter that she had written to Hugh, her story seeemed idiotic. She tore the letter up, and wrote again and did not mention the small man. Hugh, she thought, would not in any case be amused. She could not make the story amusing. She could just make it sound silly. Hugh might be interested in a man that smelled like an animal (she had seldom smelled an animal), but she would not be able to conceal from him the fact that something was being established that affected her unreasonably and unpleasantly; it seemed to her that the small man, in spite of his apparent immobility and unawareness, was in some peculiar way aware of her also. This, of course, was possible, yet unlikely and very unpleasant. She neither saw the small man, nor did the strange scent reach her, for a long time.

One night it rained. Mary drove carefully in her little car. She picked up her cousin, Cora Wilmot, and drove through the lashing rain, and through the lights and reflections of lights, cross-hatched in the early dark in splashing pools and pavements, lighted by and left behind by the beams of her own headlights, onto Granville Street Bridge. She drove carefully in the late dinner-time traffic, peering through the rainstorm. She drove rather slowly. Cora, beside her, peered too. Then the thing nearly happened.

Just before Mary reached the narrow span of the bridge, Cora cried out, and stifled her cry. Off the slightly raised platform-like sidewalk of the bridge, into the light of the headlights of Mary's slowly moving car, stepped a small man. He faced the lights of the car, and seemed to look through the windshield of the car and at, or into, the occupants. The lights showed all in one flash the white face (and Mary could see the lighted russet eyes), the intolerable propriety of mouth and chin, dark lines of hair framing the almost rectangular face. The man threw up his arms with the stiff gesture of a marionette. Mary swerved sharply to the left into whatever cars there might be, into the span, if need be, rather than touch or become involved in any way with the man who had stepped in front of her car. She did not touch him. She touched neither cars nor span. She did not speak. She drove to the end of the bridge, up Granville Street hill, through lights, darkness, and rain, and then she pulled up at the side of the road. She was trembling violently. Cora was voluble.

"That horrible little man!" she said, "*What* was he doing? *Why* did he do it? He did it on purpose! No one crosses the bridge there! There's nothing to cross for! Oh Mary, what a narrow shave! Let's sit here a while. What a face! He looked as if he could see us, as if he was looking at us! I'll never forget him, will you? Do you feel like driving now? Let's get there, and then they'll give us a drink before dinner, and that will help us both."

"Yes," said Mary, and she drove on. He saw me, she thought, as I drove so slowly in the lights, and then stepped out.

Before the end of the year, Hugh came home, the war being incredibly over. And then, as I said, Hugh went to Australia, and Mary, with the complicated fracture of her left arm in a sling, stayed at home.

Many and many a time, towards the end of the war, and now, when alone, when sleeping, and at waking, she seemed to see the doll-like figure of the small man with her motor lights full on his white face. She saw a marionette's gesture—two dark arms flung stiffly upwards, she swerved, she drove on in her dream. And then, the obsession became less frequent. Nevertheless, within herself, she knew that she had begun to be afraid of something.

Hugh wrote from Melbourne, "I'm going to be here longer than we thought. Just as soon as that elbow is better enough cable me. I'll advise you, and you get a passage by air. And at last. . . ." The load of aggravation lifted from Mary, and she began to lie about her elbow in order to get away and to join Hugh in Australia. However, their friend the doctor, Johnny Weston, put her off for a week.

One afternoon she returned from John's surgery with the permission that she might now make arrangements for her flight to Australia, and so she cabled to Hugh. Such a thing as this had never happened to Mary Manly before. She went home, and in her ecstasy, her rapture, she telephoned Thérèse Leduc and Cora, and anybody else that came to mind, to tell them that she was flying to Australia to join Hugh.

There came a ring at the door of the flat. Still careful of her clumsy left arm, Mary went lightly to the door and opened it. A feral smell entered the apartment, followed by the small respectable man who had stood outside Mary's door and had rung her doorbell. The man was dressed as usual in black. As he stepped humbly but without question into the hall, he took off his obsolete square-shaped bowler hat, laid it upon a table, turned and shut the door in a serviceable manner, and then advanced obsequiously on Mary. In his hand he carried a small black valise. Scent hung heavy and it was the smell of fear.

Mary was aghast. Her right hand flew to her mouth. She pressed the back of her hand to her mouth and gazed at the small man over her hand. She did not think, I am alone in this apartment with this unpleasant little creature. She did not think at all. The air was full of the dank wild earthy smell of something old and unknown. She backed, and obsequiously the small man advanced upon her. She saw the russet animal eyes, the reddish animal fur. She saw the prissy gentility of the lips. She smelled the smell.

"Sleepwalker," said the man softly, looking at her.

Mary snatched up a small bronze vase, and hit the man hard upon the side of the head. He looked at her with infinite surprise and reproach, swayed, and sank to the floor. He lay there like a large black-garbed doll, and blood began to flow from the wound on his head. His eyes were closed and he was very pale.

Mary stood looking down upon him, and tried to measure what she had done. "Three minutes ago," she thought, "I was mad with joy because I was going to Hugh, and now perhaps I have killed a man who is a stranger." She now felt curiously hard and not at all frightened. She went to the telephone and called John Weston at his surgery.

"John," she said, "this is Mary Manly. I am at home. I think I have killed a man. Please come." And she hung up the telephone and went back to the small man who lay as she had left him.

I am very stupid, thought Mary, because I do not know whether he is unconscious or whether he is dead, and I don't know how to find out such things. At least I will bathe his head, and perhaps if he is unconscious he will rally a bit. She got water and a cloth, and although it was repugnant to her, she knelt down and bathed the wound which she had inflicted on the small respectable man. He stirred. He opened his eyes and looked steadily at her. She rose to her feet and looked down at him.

"Dear lady," whispered the man, still prostrate on the floor, "whatever made you do that to me?" and his eyes were indeed the eyes of an animal.

Well, thought Mary, I can see that this is going to be a very odd conversation. She could not answer his question, and so she said, "I am very, very sorry that I have done this to you, but why are you here? And why did you walk into my flat like that? And what was that you said to me when you came in?" It gave her satisfaction that John Weston would soon come, and would act as some kind of a solvent to this situation.

The man sat up slowly, and felt his head. He looked at his red hand with surprise, and again looked up at Mrs. Manly.

"Name of Sleepwalker," he said, "carrying a line of ladies' underwear samples of special buys in rayon, silk, crêpe, also ladies' hosiery put out by the Silki-Silk Company with agents in all major cities of Canada," and he looked at the black valise which lay where it had fallen.

"Oh," said Mary, feeling very silly indeed. "And do you really mean that your name is Sleepwalker?"

"Name of Handel Sleepwalker," said Mr. Sleepwalker, and subsided again into a faint on the floor.

The doorbell rang, and Mary opened the door to Dr. Weston. Because Dr. Weston was ruffled, and had—unwillingly—left his patients when Mary summoned him so imperatively and strangely, he had, since leaving his consulting-room, built up a genuine and justified annoyance mixed with real uneasiness, and because he could find no other object for his annoyance, he had hung it upon Mary Manly. Therefore by the time Dr. Weston arrived at Mary's apartment he was very angry indeed with her for having killed a man at a quarter past five in the afternoon, for having taken him forcibly from his consultations, and for having chosen to do this at a time when Hugh was not at home and therefore was unable to take the matter in hand. Although a very good friend of Hugh and Mary, Dr. Weston was not at that moment in the frame of mind to shoulder the results of murder. This is why, when Mary opened the door with a sense of relief, John Weston dismayed her by a complete absence of sympathy; he turned on her an angry face, and roared at her in an injured manner, "What on earth *have* you been doing?" as if she were guilty. Well, so she was.

Mary, aware of all that had gone before that was so ridiculously unexplainable at that very instant, realized that she had to cope with her own emotions, to attend — in the first place — to Mr. Sleepwalker who lay inert on the livingroom floor, and to manage Dr. Weston either by returning anger for anger, innocence for anger, or by disregarding anger. This latter she decided to do.

"Come," she said. She turned and indicated Mr. Sleepwalker with an air quite sublime. "You see!"

When Dr. Weston saw the actual body of Mr. Sleepwalker lying on the floor of the room in which Dr. Weston and his wife had so often enjoyed a cocktail, and saw Mr. Sleepwalker's blood upon the carpet, and saw Mary standing there pale, helpless, bandaged, and gentle, other feelings began to take possession of him. He kneeled down and examined the prostrate one. Then he looked up and said to Mary in a fretful tone, "He's not dead at all!"

Well, really, thought Mary, this is too much! Does John expect that one should make sure of *killing* someone before disturbing him! John is going to be aggravating, I can see. But she said simply, "Oh, John, I am so thankful. This has been very alarming."

"Did *you* hit him?" asked Dr. Weston, scrambling to his feet.

"Oh yes, I hit him."

"Why. . . ?"

"He *terrified* me," said Mary. "He stole into the room when I opened the door, and followed me up, and did not explain his business, and then he said something that frightened me very much. And here I was with my bad arm and alone, and before I realized what I was doing, John, I hit him with that little vase."

"What did he say to you?" asked Dr. Weston.

Mr. Sleepwalker spoke from the floor. His eyes were closed. He said softly, "I did not indeed desire to frighten the dear lady; I merely told the dear lady my name."

Dr. Weston shot a very baleful look at Mary; he became suspicious of her again (and there were all those patients in the waiting-room).

"And what *is* your name?" asked Dr. Weston.

"Sleepwalker," said Mr. Sleepwalker, opening his eyes.

"And where do you live?" asked Dr. Weston.

Mr. Sleepwalker closed his eyes again. "I am afraid," he said, "that for the moment I am unable to remember."

"Well, where would you like us to take you?" asked the doctor.

"Yes, where would you like us to take you?" asked Mary, eagerly.

Mr. Sleepwalker paused for a moment. Then, "I would like to stay ere," he said.

"That is impossible, quite impossible," said Dr. Weston crossly. "You can take him to the hospital, Mary. He's all right to move, and a day or two will be all that's needed."

"John," said Mary, taking the doctor aside, "do you notice a very queer smell in this room?"

"No, I don't," said the doctor. "Do you?"

She did not answer. "I will get an ambulance if you will arrange with the hospital," she said.

"I would much prefer," said a silky voice from the floor, "if the dear lady would take me to the ospital erself. Far be it indeed to go in an ambulance."

Mary scowled at the doctor, who said at once, "No, we'll get an ambulance. See if you can sit up now."

Mr. Sleepwalker obediently sat up, a little black figure with legs outstretched on the floor. The doctor supported him.

"Now into this chair."

"I am a poor man," said Mr. Sleepwalker, sitting up straight and stiff in the chair, with his disfigured head.

"I will pay for your ambulance, Mr. Sleepwalker, and I will pay for your days in the hospital as long as Dr. Weston says that you must stay," said Mary.

"Oh, ow kind, dear lady," said Mr. Sleepwalker humbly, and Mary thought, What a brute I am, I've never abased myself and really apologized for hitting him! "I shall get you some tea," she said. Meanwhile, the doctor was busy at the telephone. He looked at his watch. "Don't leave me!" murmured Mary as she brushed past him in the hall, and Dr. Weston gave her an unaffectionate look. She took a tray in to Mr. Sleepwalker, who gazed round the room as though he were memorizing it.

"I shall burn this tray, break the cup and saucer, give away the chair, and send the carpet to the cleaners, or we can sell it—in fact, we might leave the flat. I can't bear to have had this little horror in the room," Mary said to herself unfairly, forgetting that she was very lucky.

Mr. Sleepwalker coughed. "One thing may I hask," he said.

"What?" said Mary.

"I should like to hask," he said, "that the dear lady will visit me in the ospital."

Mary considered. That was the very least she could do.

"Yes, of course I will," she said, trying to sound hearty.

"Oh, thank you, *thank* you," said Mr. Sleepwalker. The doctor came out of the hall.

"I have arranged for the bed and the ambulance," he said, looking again at his watch. "Some time I will hear more about this." He had one leg out of the door.

"You will stay!" besought Mary with agitation, seizing his arm.

The doctor put down his overcoat again. "Very well, I will stay," he said irritably, and thought of his waiting-room. He did not like Mary Manly at all just now, whether because she had or had not killed Mr. Sleepwalker (although on the whole he was relieved that she had not); but chiefly he disliked Mary because she had behaved in an irrational manner—he disapproved of people being irrational—and had called him away from his surgery in the middle of the afternoon. He whirled to the telephone, and Mary heard him say brusquely, "I'll be back.

Keep Mrs. Jenkins, and tell Mr. Howe I'll see him tomorrow, and explain to the two others that I'll see them tomorrow, and give them a time, and tell Mrs. Boniface that I'll drop in on the way home, and don't let the Jackson boy go home till I've seen him, and. . . ."

"Oh Lord," thought Mary, contrite, "what have I done to all these people! Poor Johnny!" and she tried to look pathetic, but it was no good.

The ambulance arrived, and Dr. Weston sped away. Two burly ambulance men helped Mr. Sleepwalker; he walked between them in his still fashion. One big man carried his absurdly small valise. The other one took charge of the obsolete hat. Mary stood.

At the door Mr. Sleepwalker made as if to turn.

"I do hask, dear lady, that you will recollect your promise?" he said, with a question.

"I will indeed," said Mary heartily and with the greatest repugnance.

She heard the door close. She turned and opened all the windows, and did what she could to the room. Then she telephoned Cora. "Cora," she said, "a very peculiar thing has happened. I won't tell you over the telephone, but here, but for the grace of God, sits your cousin, the famous murderess . . . " a thought checked her, "or," and she laughed, "the famous huntress."

"What *do* you mean!" asked Cora.

"Well," said Mary slowly, "you remember the night we nearly ran that man down on the bridge?"

"Yes, yes," said Cora.

"Well," continued Mary slowly, "it's the same man. Coincidence, of course, of the most extraordinary kind" (was it coincidence?) "and it's left me rather shaken."

"Too much happens to you. Come at once and have dinner," said Cora.

"I will," said Mary gratefully.

As Mary Manly went to her cousin's house, she asked herself some questions. If I wished to go the bottom of the queerness of this, if I had any scientific curiosity and not just a detestation of the whole affair, I would take up a notebook and pencil, and question that . . . that . . . person (she avoided even his name). I would say to him, Was your aunt a fox, or was your grandmother a weasel, and of course, he would say no, and where should I find myself then? I could ask him if he seeks me in particular, and how, and why. But I am such a coward that I don't want to know. Then I would say, My good sir, do you know that you smell? And if he said yes, I should have to ask him, Do some people (such as I) and not other people, recognize this animal (yes, I should have to say "animal") scent? I can see how totally impossible such a conversation is, and so I shall leave it alone, and shall admit, to myself, and not to others, only the fact that this man frightens me. . . .

When Mary left Cora the next morning (for Cora easily persuaded her to stay the night), she knew that the talk of her attack upon Mr. Sleepwalker would spread among her friends and acquaintances, and that it would be well and properly launched by Cora. She realized that she would be the object of universal pity ("Poor Mrs. Manly, wasn't it dreadful for her! The man, my dear, walked straight into the flat, and there was Mary all alone, with a broken arm. . . . I think she's very good not to prosecute! And so brave. The most extraordinary coincidence my dear! Cora Wilmot says. . . . ") and that this was not quite fair to Mr. Sleepwalker who, after all, was the one who had been hit on the temple with a bronze vase and was now in hospital. She knew that she would be decried as soft, foolish, and too kind because she had provided the ambulance and was about to pay the hospital bill. However, she had to choose between all or nothing, and the section of the story which was in Cora's possession, and which Cora would launch on all their acquaintances with her well-known energy, approximated to nothing, and that was best.

The following afternoon Mary said to herself as she alighted clumsily with parcels at the hospital, This (calling on this man, I mean) is the most unpleasant thing that I have deliberately done in my whole life. I don't call hitting . . . Mr.

Sleepwalker . . . deliberate. It was instinctive. If only Hugh were with me it would be easier. However, as she had that afternoon received a cable from Hugh which read: "Cheers and cheers take first passage and cable me", she felt more carefree than she would have thought possible. I can tell this . . . individual . . . she thought, that I am going to Australia (that seems far enough away)—which is true—that I'm going tomorrow, which is not true, but it is true enough. And she entered the hospital.

She found Mr. Sleepwalker propped up a little on his pillows, looking very pale. His head was bandaged, and when she saw the bandage, she felt much more guilty than when, in the storm of terror, she had struck down Mr. Sleepwalker and had seen him lying on the floor, with blood flowing upon the carpet.

Patients in the adjacent beds regarded her apathetically. Mr. Sleepwalker looked earnestly, too earnestly, at her. I should, of course, give him my hand, she said to herself, this hand which has struck him down. But she did not wish to do so. She found that her feelings were strangely involved. In order to avoid touching Mr. Sleepwalker's hand, and for no more altruistic reason, Mary had filled her good hand with flowers, and carried magazines and a box of chocolates under her arm. As she disposed these articles awkwardly about Mr. Sleepwalker's bed, the handshaking moment passed, as she had intended it should. A nurse, seeing her arm in a sling, brought forward a chair. Mary smiled at her, thanked her, and sat down.

"I hope you are not too uncomfortable," she said.

"Oh, no, thank you, dear lady," said Mr. Sleepwalker. "this is a very nice ospital, nicer than what I was in in England that time the dogs bit me."

"Dogs . . . !" said Mary.

"Ounds," said Mr. Sleepwalker.

Mr. Sleepwalker's bandages really afflicted Mary. They made her feel more guilty even than her own conscience. However, she could not afford to get soft about Mr. Sleepwalker, even though she had hit him with a vase.

"I am sorry that I cannot have a nice long chat," she said untruthfully, "but the fact is that I am flying to Australia tomorrow to join my husband."

"Come a little closer, dear lady," said Mr. Sleepwalker. His reddish eyes were fixed upon her. Mary made hitching noises with her chair, but she was near enough. She began to feel faint. "I should like to go to Australia," he said. "Oh, ow I should like!"

"Australia is, I am sure, a very nice country," replied Mary with considerable idiocy. I must keep this impersonal, she thought, and proceeded to talk about Australia, of which she knew very little. "So you see I cannot stay any longer; in fact, I must go. Everything will be arranged, the bill, you know. I am so very sorry for what I did to you. It was really some terrible misunderstanding."

The little man in the bed continued to look earnestly at her.

"It as been a pleasure indeed to meet you, dear lady," he said in his soft voice. (What an extraordinary statement! thought Mary.) "May I thank you indeed for your kindness, and may I tell you, dear lady, ow grateful I ave always been to you, and ow I ave frequently and in oh ever so many places enjoyed your delicious smell . . . fragrance, I *should* say."

"My. . . ! my. . . !" stammered Mary, and sprang to her feet. She stood for one moment looking down at Mr. Sleepwalker. Then she turned and the patients saw her running like a hare out of the ward.

ACKNOWLEDGEMENTS

ROBERTSON DAVIES: "The Cat That Went to Trinity", from *One Half of Robertson Davies* (Toronto: Macmillan Company of Canada Ltd., 1977). Reprinted by permission of the author.

H.R. PERCY: "The Timeless Island", from *The Timeless Island and Other Stories* (Toronto: The Ryerson Press, 1960). First published in *Vanity Fair* (U.K.).
Copyright © H.R. Percy. Reprinted by permission of the author.

HUGH GARNER: "The Premeditated Death of Samuel Glover", from *The Yellow Sweater and Other Stories* (Toronto: William Collins & Sons, 1953). Reprinted by permission of McGraw-Hill Ryerson Limited.

YVES THERIAULT: "The Barren Field", from *Weird Tales*, November 1949.
Copyright © 1949 by Yves Thériault. Reprinted by permission of the author.

GRAHAM PETRIE: "Village Theatre", from *Story Quarterly*, Winter, 1975.
Copyright © 1975 by *Story Quarterly.* Reprinted by permission of the author.

AL PURDY: "The Undertaker", from *The Canadian Forum*, October 1962.

Copyright © 1962 by Al Purdy. Reprinted by permission of the author.

BRIAN MOORE: "The Sight", from *Irish Ghost Stories* (London: Hamish Hamilton, 1977), edited by Joseph Hone.

P.K. PAGE: "The Woman", from *The Sun and the Moon and Other Fictions* (Toronto: House of Anansi, 1973).

WILFRED WATSON: "The Lice", from *Prism International*, Fall 1960.

Copyright © 1960 by Wilfred Watson. Reprinted by permission of the author.

MICHEL TREMBLAY: "The Thirteenth Wife of Baron Klugg", from *Stories for Late-Night Drinkers* (Vancouver: Intermedia Press, 1977), translated by Michael Bullock.

LAWRENCE MATHEWS: "The Death of Arthur Rimbaud", from *Canadian Fiction Magazine*, Spring 1975.

Copyright © 1975 by Lawrence Mathews. Reprinted by permission of the author.

ANDREAS SCHROEDER: "The Late Man", from *The Late Man and Other Fictions* (Victoria: Sono Nis Press, 1972).

ETHEL WILSON: "Mr. Sleepwalker", from *Mrs. Golightly and Other Stories* (Toronto: Macmillan and Company Ltd., 1961).